CLUB OF CONTENTS

Trigger Warning:

This novel contains sexual situations described in vivid detail. This novel contains discussions that reference violence and abuse. Reader discretion is advised.

CHAPTER ONE
Newbie

"Please… it can't possibly be all of that," Chamere spits out in an unbelieving tone. Her new roommates, Beyonka and Erica, glare at her weirdly.

"Bey, she must not have heard a thing we said," Erica states dryly as she applies more lipstick to her already crimson lips. Chamere curiously proceeds to Erica's small vanity to glare at her impressive makeup collection.

"I did hear what y'all said, it's just a little hard to believe, that's all. Plus, I did an internet search on the place, and it doesn't seem all that appealing. If you've seen one club, you've seen em' all." Erica and Beyonka expel identical sighs.

"You'll just have to see what we mean-"

"Because seeing is believing," they say in unison. Beyonka adjusts her perky boobs in her black sheer shirt as she studies her undeniable redbone beauty in Erica's floor-length mirror. Chamere stands behind her, glancing at her simple outfit consisting of blue jeans, a purple V-neck tee and a pair of gym shoes. She eventually concludes that she is either underdressed for tonight or these chicks are doing too much for a lame ass club.

She secretly decides on the latter.

"Are you sure you don't want to change? I told you; I have a cute little dress hanging in my closet that would be so gorgeous on you," Beyonka blurts out as soon as she spots Chamere's reflection behind hers. She spins around to face her with coercing eyes. Chamere looks away awkwardly.

"That's OK, Beyonka, but thanks anyway. Skimpy stuff ain't really my style." Beyonka looks slightly disappointed.

"Leave her alone, Bey. Can't you tell she's going for the safe and comfortable look," Erica utters in a mocking tone. Chamere rolls her eyes at her.

"There's nothing wrong with dressing casually, especially when I'm only going to some hole-in-the-wall club that no one outside of this hick town has heard of." Erica rapidly spins around in her vanity chair to broadcast the offended expression painted on her cocoa brown face. It's evident that Chamere's words rubbed her the wrong way.

Erica folds her arms, "I swear… city folks kill me thinking they are so much better than we are. If Chicago is such an amazing place, then why are you renting a room in our little ole country house, then? Why leave all your friends and family in a big city to settle in this dark corner of Alabama, Ms. Thang?"

Erica and Beyonka glare at Chamere as if they are impatiently waiting for an explanation. Every time the ladies ask Chamere about "home", she conveniently changes the subject. She has avoided talking about what happened in Chicago for two months and she's not planning on spilling the beans now. Chamere swallows the lump of embarrassment growing in her throat. She instantly backs off.

"My bad, y'all. I didn't mean to shit on y'all hometown. That was not my intention," she exclaims as apologetically as possible. Erica smacks her lips before returning to her previous position.

Chamere hurries to change the subject, "So, what time are we leaving? It's almost midnight and you chicks ain't even ready yet." Erica ignores Chamere on purpose, obligating Beyonka to answer her question.

"There's no rush. Ain't nothing that interesting happening at the club right now, anyway. Believe me when I tell you… the real fun doesn't begin until the clock strikes 2am."

$$$

"Club Liquor," Chamere mumbles to herself, reading the neon sign illuminating the night sky above the large building. Her mouth gapes open at the sight of several groups of people lingering around the club. "Shit, that's a lot of folks."

"Don't we know it," Erica replies in an irritated tone. "This is the best low-key club in the tri-state area." She parks her red Malibu in the first available spot she sees. Chamere sits patiently in the backseat while Erica and Beyonka stare at their foundation-covered faces in their visor mirrors. After a light primp, the ladies climb out of the car.

"Be careful, Bey. You nearly fall every time we come here," Erica warns as soon as their high heels sink into the dirt road considered to be a parking lot. The uneven feel of the gravel underneath Beyonka's feet makes her knees buckle.

"Hold on to me," Chamere insists with an outreach of her arm. Beyonka grabs it immediately. "See; I guess it wasn't a bad idea to dress comfortably after all," she spits out, making an obvious reference to Erica's earlier teasing. She extends her other arm towards Erica, but she ignores her friendly gesture altogether.

"Welcome to ladies' night," Chamere whispers after reading the ground sign positioned near the club's entrance. "Ladies get in free until 11pm. Hours of operation: 9pm – 2am." Chamere taps Beyonka on the arm, "Hey, the sign says that this place closes at 2am. I thought you said that's when the party starts?" Erica and Beyonka giggle at Chamere's ignorance as they sashay past the club's door. They proceed to the dark alley behind the building. Chamere's confusion grows tenfold.

"Ladies, seriously… what the hell is going on? We just passed the door-"

"You'll find out," Erica replies vaguely. They silently step through the tight space until a neon sign can be seen through the darkness. "By Invitation Only" flashes above a single black door directly in front of them. Chamere glares behind her when she hears footsteps other than theirs. She spots a herd of women turning down the alley to follow them.

"By invitation only? But I don't have an invitation," Chamere notes. Erica reaches into her clutch purse and pulls out a small card. She hands it to Chamere.

"You didn't… but you do now."

CHAPTER TWO
By Invitation Only

Chamere examines the small black card with bewildered eyes. Outside of the words, "Visitor's Pass", displayed in obnoxious white letters across the front of it and a weird logo in the bottom right-hand corner, there is nothing else present on the card.

"Ladies, I'm really trying my best not to freak out here. I don't do surprises, I hate escape rooms, and if you bitches are trying to kill me, I swear to God I'll haunt y'all every fucking night-"

The door opening suddenly puts a fork in Chamere's nervous rant. The sound of sexy rhythm and blues music melodically fills her ears. The sight of the big, burly man stepping through the dark doorway causes Chamere to take a startled step back. Every woman in attendance immediately digs inside of their purses as if they're searching for something. Eventually, each lady has a gold card in their grasp. Erica holds hers up for the guy to see. He gives her a single head nod, signaling for her to proceed through the door. Beyonka tugs Chamere towards the man.

"She's our guest," Beyonka states with a flash of her card. He stares at Chamere with cold eyes. "Your card--- give it to him," Beyonka whispers while elbowing Chamere in the side. Chamere clumsily hands the card to the scary man. His single head nod grants them access across the threshold.

"What the…" Chamere starts, pausing as soon as the interior of the mysterious place comes into view. The sinister, but sexy ambience catches her completely off guard.

It looks like a rumpus room for freaks.

Beyonka proceeds to guide Chamere further inside as more women pile in behind them. The dark romance themed décor gives the lusty space a naughty vibe. Not to mention, the sea of shirtless men standing against the far wall nearly takes her breath away. They stand perfectly still as if they are robots awaiting activation. She had no idea there were so many versions of fine until her eyes took in each and every one of them. Her lips part in shock. "Where--- I mean, what---"

"Welcome to ladies' night," Beyonka informs her with a huge grin. Erica tosses her hand up and gestures for the ladies to join her near the center of the hedonistic lair. They move in her direction.

"I must admit, I am so confused right now. What is this place?" Chamere inquires over the mood music. Her curious eyes continue to take in the debaucherous scenery while waiting for either lady to respond.

"It's Club Liquor," Erica responds facetiously. Chamere rolls her eyes at her.

"I've gathered that much, Erica. It's just that the stuff I found on the internet about this place failed to mention the sex dungeon we're currently standing in."

"That's because this part of the club doesn't exist," Erica speaks again. Chamere huffs as if she's starting to annoy her.

"She's right, Chamere. Technically, this room doesn't exist… at least, we're supposed to act like it doesn't."

"I don't understand," Chamere admits. Beyonka glances at the chatty women standing near them.

"This is a club within a club; one that we are sworn to secrecy to be a part of; one that requires an invitation to even know about-"

"One that provides us with more pleasure than we can handle," Erica adds in an erotic octave. Beyonka nods her head seductively as if she agrees.

"It sounds and looks like a male brothel," Chamere points out after glancing at the half-naked men in jeans again. It's apparent to Chamere that the guys are here to perform some sort of raunchy act. Erica displeasingly shakes her head at Chamere's assumption while Beyonka wrestles with the unfavorable comparison.

"Those gorgeous men over there are not prostitutes and this is most definitely not a brothel. This is a secret after-party that was created strictly to cater to and pamper women."

"Really? And how legal is this?" Erica sucks her teeth at Chamere's inappropriate question.

"Why do you have to bring legalities into this? Every lady here is here because she wants to be. We don't speak about this experience outside of these walls. We will never chance the authorities shutting it down. This place is that damn addicting." Chamere chuckles to herself. She can't believe how desperate Erica is sounding right now. It makes sense in a way, though.

Where would exotic dancers be without their groupies?

Chamere looks turned off, "I don't know, y'all. I've always hated strip clubs. This might not be for me."

"Why am I not surprised?" Erica mumbles under her breath. She turns to address Beyonka, "I told you this was a mistake."

Chamere smacks her lips, "And what is that supposed to mean?"

Beyonka intervenes, "This is far from a strip club, Chamere. Come on girl, just give it a chance. Your visitor's pass is good for one night only, anyway. You'd have to join the club if you wanted to come back. Try to have a good time."

Chamere sighs with a fold of her arms, "Fine… I'll try."

CHAPTER THREE
Skirts

"Ladies, ladies, ladies…" the women hear from over the loudspeakers. Chamere jumps when the deep voice startles her. "We've been waiting all week to see your beautiful faces again. We can't wait to service your every want, need, and desire. Your wishes are our commands. Welcome to ladies' night."

The entire room erupts with the approval of the excited women. Chamere's face is covered with uneasiness when the men step away from the wall. She grabs Beyonka's arm tightly. Beyonka loosens her grasp, "Chamere, you need to relax. They're not about to murder us."

Chamere releases Beyonka's arm after her words embarrass her. She's a Chicago girl; she's not supposed to be afraid of anything. She straightens up as the men get closer to them.

"Wait a second fellas… hold on," the voice over the loudspeaker blurts out, causing the men to halt in their tracks. Each one of them remain in a horizontal line like sexy soldiers awaiting battle. They are so close to the women that Chamere can smell the hypnotizing oil they have smeared all over their bulging muscles.

The light-skinned man directly in front of her takes in her body with his hazel eyes. His cowboy hat and long beard make him look like a ghetto rancher. His well-defined chest flexes once he has her attention. She swallows hard when his masculinity intimidates her.

"Dino, where you at?" The voice continues. The women shout as if they know exactly where Dino is. The fine guy standing in front of Beyonka grins, revealing his award-winning smile. The deep dimples that accompany it are the icing on a sexy ass slice of caramel cake.

"What up, Liyan?" He roars to the eye in the sky.

"Aye… how are we looking down there? Are we at buffet status tonight?" Dino glares at every woman in attendance. He slowly licks his lips, "Hell yeah. They all look good enough to eat." Each woman blushes like he is talking about them personally. Liyan chuckles.

"Mm… well I guess I should come down there and check out the food options myself." The women react favorably to Liyan's declaration. Suddenly, a door swings open at the top of a shadowy staircase. The women scream louder when Liyan eases down them. He steps into the light, revealing his tall frame layered in expensive business attire. His blue suit and tie getup, even though very appealing, makes him look slightly overdressed for the occasion.

"Ladies," he greets them with a gorgeous smile. His well-trimmed goatee and sideburns connect to some of the best-looking waves Chamere has ever seen. He slaps fives with Dino before speaking into the lavalier microphone affixed to his collar, "Shit, you ain't lying. These ladies came to tease us tonight. I really hope some of them are willing to give us what we're craving."

Some women raise their hands while others fan themselves. Beyonka and Erica nudge each other happily. They glance at Chamere, who appears too taken aback to react to anything that is going on right now. Her dumbfounded expression says it all.

"So, Dino--- who do you have your eye on tonight?" Dino steps out of line like he's deep in thought. He begins to pace the small space between the men and women. He pauses in front of Chamere, causing her to nearly wet herself. He smirks at how unstable he's making her.

"Well, I'm kinda in the mood for a skirt tonight. I need a woman that came ready to cum." Chamere's sights immediately go to the women's attire. Nearly all of them are wearing a skirt or dress. Even the ones that aren't are sporting tiny shorts or skintight leggings. She is the only one rocking boring ass jeans.

Is that why Beyonka was trying so hard to get her to change clothes?

"Yeah, Dino… that really narrows it down," Liyan exclaims jokingly. The ladies giggle like smitten schoolgirls. Dino laughs, too.

"OK, well, I'm not going to lie… I did taste someone last week and I can't stop thinking about her flavor. She creamed down my throat so good; I think I want some more of her." Erica nearly rips Beyonka's arm off after Dino's words. He approaches her seductively. "The scent of you lingered on my face, even after we went our separate ways. I miss the shit out of your pheromones. Can you feed me that pussy again?"

Dino sticks his hand out for Erica, and she doesn't hesitate to take it. He swings her arm around his body and places it on his shoulder. They move towards a red leather couch in the corner with his arm snuggly around her waist.

"Bey, what is happening right now? I know he's not about to do what I think he is," Chamere questions Beyonka in an alarmed tone. Beyonka grins at Chamere's shocked state.

"Of course he is. They don't call this 'Club Lick Her' for nothing."

CHAPTER FOUR
Club Lick Her

Chamere watches closely as Dino and Erica approach the sofa. He gently spins her around to face him. He whispers something in her ear that tickles her fancy. She's laughing when Dino proceeds to his knees.

Erica gawks at Dino in amazement while he submits himself to her. He slides his hands up her chocolate thighs and slowly shimmies down her satin panty. She steps out of them before easing down on the couch. Her smooth legs spread right in front of his face.

He admires her freshly waxed pussy by exploring it with his hands. He licks his lips before licking her sweet spot. He slurps on her vagina with nearly perfect precision. She shivers from his passionate skills. The sound of her moaning acts as an official party starter.

"Fellas, the floor is yours. Treat these women just like they want to be treated," Liyan demands. He steps back to expose the wolf pack to their prey. Chamere moves backwards while the other women step forward.

She's not sure if she can handle something like this.

"Hey, are you OK," Beyonka asks after noticing the distress covering Chamere's face. Chamere gestures that she isn't. Beyonka leads her to the bar, which is displaying a "complimentary drinks" sign in large letters. She asks the bartender for a cup of water.

"Look, I'm really sorry, Chamere. I didn't think you would get this upset about ladies' night. I thought you would enjoy yourself, actually." She shakes her head, "Fuck! Now I owe Erica 20 bucks." Chamere nearly spits out her water.

"What? Why would you owe Erica 20 bucks?"

"Because I bet her that you wouldn't freak out. I guess I was wrong." Chamere seems bothered by Beyonka's confession. There is something about Erica discrediting her that makes her blood boil. She slams the cup of water on the bar.

"I'm not freaked out! I'm just… I mean, things… this place just caught me off guard, that's all." Beyonka nods her head like she's buying Chamere's bullshit. They ease into a pair of bar stools.

"I feel you. I think I went to the bathroom with bubble guts the first time Erica brought me here. I couldn't believe that these fine ass men were running around here at our beck and call. It's still unbelievable-"

"What is?" Mr. Ghetto Rancher jumps in their conversation to ask. Beyonka blushes after taking in his unexpected and gorgeous presence.

"I was talking about the misters here. This is my friend's first time." He turns his attention towards Chamere.

"I kinda figured you were new here. You don't look like someone I've tasted before."

"Whoa, slow your roll, Stallion. She's having a hard time processing all of this as it is. Don't scare her away." Stallion removes his hat and tips it respectfully, revealing his crispy braids underneath. The sound of Erica cumming snatches Beyonka and Chamere's attention from Stallion to her loud sounds of ecstasy. They spot Dino munching between Erica's legs like it's their wedding night. She tries to push him away, but he's locked on to her clit so tightly that she can hardly move.

"She can't fight him off. She tried last week and failed miserably."

"That's Dino for you. He doesn't know when to quit. I take the gentler approach myself. I'm not torturous. If you want me to stop, then say the word," Stallion mentions. His eyes sexily devour Beyonka's being. Beyonka smirks.

"I know how you do, Stallion; I had you last month."

"And you didn't come back to me? Damn, I must've been awful, then. Ouch, that hurts." He rests his hand on his chiseled chest as if his heart is broken. Beyonka giggles.

"Perhaps you were so good that I had to jump ship before I got hooked." Stallion takes a dominating step towards her.

"Why don't you sit on my face right now until we figure out which one it is?" Beyonka eagerly hops up from her seat. She disappears with Stallion as if she forgot all about her chat with Chamere. Chamere turns to face the bartender.

"I need a double scotch--- scratch that, give me the whole damn bottle since drinks are free here."

"Are we celebrating something?" Chamere hears from behind her. She immediately recognizes the voice as the one blaring from the overhead speakers earlier. She sighs before turning to face him.

She pauses like she forgot how handsome he was, "Umm… nothing but the death of my social life."

"Wow, that sounds dramatic," he points out while sitting next to her. He signals for the bartender to slide him a glass. "No point in drinking an entire bottle of scotch alone. I'll help." She makes an uninterested face.

"No offense, but I can be a party pooper by myself."

"You can't poop on my party if you tried… this ain't that type of bar." He laughs but Chamere doesn't. He pours him a shot and chugs it, "Tough crowd." He tries to engage with her, "Something is telling me that you don't like my club."

"What's there to like?" Chamere challenges Liyan with a serious look. The silence he allows to linger magnifies the mountains of moans over baby-making music in the background.

"Evidently, plenty." Chamere eats her words to regurgitate her point.

"I meant, this is odd… and not to mention, unsanitary."

"Odd? I don't think so. You can find bars up and down the west coast that do the exact same things; and unsanitary? Not at all. Sure, we swap bodily fluids, but

STD tests are administered every month by our registered clinician. We take health very seriously around here."

"Well, where is your clinician now? I'm here and I haven't been tested."

"Testing is for members only, but something is telling me that I don't have to worry about you signing on that dotted line any time soon."

"Not in a million years," Chamere states in a mostly believable tone. Liyan grins at her. He sticks his hand out for her to shake.

"Well, it was still nice to meet you…" he pauses as if he's waiting for her to tell him her name.

"Chamere."

"Chamere," he repeats, "I'm Liyan." Her palm connects with his. His beautiful brown eyes delve into hers, "And if I may ask: Can you please refrain from mentioning this place to anyone? I want to uphold the integrity of ladies' night and keep my women happy."

"Don't worry, Liyan; your secret is safe with me," Chamere assures him. He lifts her hand towards his mouth and kisses it. The feeling of his soft lips against her skin causes a twinge between her legs that she hasn't felt in a long time. He downs another shot for the road. He turns to face her before walking away.

"It's too bad, too. I would have hung up my suit and tie and handled you personally."

CHAPTER FIVE
Liyan, the Businessman

"Bullshit! Liyan would never say that. He's the owner, not a mister," Erica spits out in a nastier tone than she intended. She tries to scale back her feistiness, but there is something about Chamere that brings out the worst in her.

Chamere humps her shoulders as if she doesn't care if Erica believes her or not, "What reason would I have to lie?"

Beyonka jumps in, "I think she's telling the truth, Erica. While Dino was serving you up, Liyan was at the bar talking to her. I've never seen Liyan stay out of his office that long." Erica smacks her lips.

"But saying that he'll eat her out? Come on, now… have you ever heard Liyan talk like that?" Beyonka doesn't appear to have an answer to Erica's question. Erica takes her silence as personal validation, "Exactly. He was probably trying to get her to buy a membership, but he's clearly barking up the wrong tree." Chamere cuts her eyes at Erica. Erica smirks, "Speaking of that: Bey, you lost the bet, so where's my 20 bucks, homie?"

Chamere glares at Erica furiously, "You know what, Erica? That's really fucked up what y'all did. Betting on me? That's some weird ass shit."

Erica humps her shoulders this time, "Ain't nothing wrong with a wager between friends. Besides, I was right, wasn't I? You can't handle a mister, let alone a man like Liyan. You will never fit in a place like that."

Chamere angrily stands from the table with her empty cereal bowl in her hand. She storms into the kitchen to wash her used dishes. She's not sure what Erica's problem is with her, but she's getting really tired of her ass. As soon as she saves up enough money for a better place, she's moving.

She doesn't need this shit from some thirsty country bitch.

"Pay her no mind. She's just mad that her period is scheduled to interrupt the next ladies' night," Beyonka says from behind Chamere. Chamere doesn't bother turning around to face her. "And if ladies' night ain't for you, then that's perfectly OK. There's no shame in that. It's an acquired taste… believe me."

"I don't get it, Bey. Doesn't it freak you out to have some dude's mouth on you that was just on some other chick? Like, that shit is disgusting."

Beyonka shrugs, "I've had boyfriends that were literally kissing me after secretly coming from some other broad's house. It happens, but at least I know what I'm getting myself into at Club Liquor. Besides, my exes were nowhere near as fine as the misters are." Chamere sighs after Beyonka's words.

Sure, she may have a point, but still…

"I hear you, Bey, but I can't bring myself to allow some random ass dude between my legs without some sort of relationship first; I don't give a damn how fine he is. Like, do y'all even know these guys' real names?"

"Of course we do. We see many of them in town all the time; and yes, Stallion's real name is Stallion. He was raised on a farm or some shit." Chamere can't help but laugh. Beyonka laughs, too, "What I'm trying to say is that, even though Erica is acting like a bitch right now, we get it. If you don't want to go to Club Liquor anymore, then we won't judge you. All that we ask is you not judge us for wanting to."

$$\$\$\$$$

Chamere hates her job, but it provides a paycheck. Plus, it will help her get away from that witch, Erica, a lot quicker. That fact alone gives her the motivation she needs to deal with her store's strange customers. She wears her fake smile for hours like an annoying Halloween mask.

"Will that be all, sir?" she asks the peculiar gentleman standing in front of her. His stringy hair and dingy clothes suggest that he rarely showers. He lowers his sunglasses to get a better look at her.

"I don't know. That all depends on if you're willing to jot down my number or not."

She tries her best not to roll her eyes, "I'm sorry, sir, but taking personal info from a customer is strictly prohibited; store policy."

"Damn, I would have rocked your world, too." Chamere frowns. He pauses out of the blue, "Shit! I forgot to grab some toilet tissue. I'll be right back." He disappears from her register like his ass in on fire. Chamere giggles at the way he runs.

"Hello again," she hears once the next customer steps up. She gasps when she sees Liyan's handsome face. He unfastens his tailored suit jacket, revealing a button-up that subtly hints towards his athletic body underneath. He smiles at her as if he's happy to see her.

"Hi," she mumbles, trying her best to hide her attraction to him. He places his random items in front of her register.

"I didn't know you worked at the drugstore," he mentions, making Chamere feel embarrassed.

"Yeah. I have to pay the bills somehow, right?"

"Hey, I respect the hustle. Before I was a businessman, I worked at a chicken joint. I smelled like fried food everywhere I went." He makes Chamere laugh.

"Wow. It sounds like you smelled delicious."

"I did… just like you did the other night."

Liyan's flirtatious words catch her completely off guard. She clears her throat awkwardly, "So, you're a businessman, huh?"

He smirks, "Yup. My partners and I own a few clubs. You might have heard of them; Club Liquor?"

Chamere shakes her head sarcastically, "Nope. Never heard of it." They both grin.

"Oh, really? You've never heard of it, huh?" They chuckle this time.

"Look--- Chamere…" he acts like he's reading her name tag even though he already knows her name. "How about you be my personal guest at Club Liquor next week?

I would love to show you a good time." Chamere begins ringing up his items after her last customer returns. She tallies up his total.

"I don't know, sir. I may be busy that night," she states as seriously as she can. He slides her another 'visitor's pass' card. She glares at it.

"I can understand that. Like I said, I'm a businessman so I respect the grind; but, if you happen to be available, you should come out for ladies' night. I promise, it'll be worth your while." He winks his eye at her sexually. She swallows the lust that is suddenly creeping up her throat.

"Umm, your total is $95.87." Liyan reaches for his wallet. He hands her his black card. His baller status secretly impresses her. Chamere rips the receipt from the printer after his payment is processed. She extends it towards Liyan. He grabs her hand and his proof of purchase simultaneously. He caresses her skin.

"I left my personal number on the back of the card. Don't hesitate to call me if you have questions about anything. I can fix almost any problem you may have." The sparks between them dissipate when his hand leaves hers. Liyan is obviously interested in Chamere and she's not sure how to handle it.

"Thank you, sir. Have a nice day." His captivating smile appears before he walks away. She places the visitor's pass in her pocket once he does.

The previous customer steps up, "Strictly prohibited, my ass!"

Chamere looks confused, "I'm sorry?"

"Don't 'I'm sorry' me, lady! It was prohibited for you to take my personal info but not his?"

She quickly thinks of an excuse, "Sir, are you open for business?"

He looks confused, "Opened for business? What are you talking about?"

"I mean, I can't take personal information, but I can take business info. He was a businessman, and I may just be his next customer."

CHAPTER SIX
Big Fish

"I still can't believe he gave you another visitor's pass," Beyonka blurts out while she and Chamere get ready for ladies' night. They are getting dressed in Beyonka's room since Erica is sitting this one out.

Chamere tries her best not to blush. "I know, right. Even though I'm going, I don't think I'll be participating. I don't know… I still think the whole concept is kinda weird," she tries to convince herself more than Beyonka. Honestly, she's not sure how she feels about ladies' night anymore.

Liyan is single-handedly changing her mind.

Beyonka responds after she's satisfied with her lipstick placement, "I can tell by the leggings you're wearing that you're not interested in anyone playing between your legs tonight. They're most definitely a step up from those damn jeans, though." Both ladies giggle, "But I get it. At the very least, go for the free liquor; and Liyan will be there. I know you want to see him again. Hell, I know I would if I were you."

Chamere appears uncertain, "I don't know, Bey. Is it really smart to continue to entertain a man that is clearly out of my league? Like Erica said, he's probably just playing nice to get another customer."

Beyonka shakes her head as if she disagrees, "I seriously doubt that. Liyan is rolling in dough, so I don't think he's too pressed over a measly membership. Plus, I've never heard of a woman receiving two visitor's passes before. He seems to really want you around, and that has to count for something."

Beyonka walks away from Chamere to tackle her finishing touches. Chamere takes a deep breath and stares at herself in the mirror. She's showing a little more cleavage than usual, and she even put on lipstick just in case Beyonka is right.

Is Liyan really interested in her?

$$$

Stepping through the door of Club Liquor's secret lust haven has Chamere's stomach in knots. The fine men that she worked so hard to get out of her mind are now standing against the wall in an extremely distracting fashion. She and Beyonka post up at the spot they were standing in during their last visit.

"Shit, Bey. Why am I so nervous?" Chamere asks rhetorically.

Beyonka answers anyway, "Because, you like Liyan and this is the only way you think you will see him. You still haven't used his number, have you?" Chamere shakes her head to confirm Beyonka's assumption. Beyonka looks disappointed, "And you just gave the card to Big Bubba so now it's gone forever."

Chamere smirks, "Actually…" she pulls out her phone, presses a button and shows Beyonka her contacts list. "I saved his number the day I got it. I'm not stupid." The friends giggle.

"I'm glad you're not, because if you let an opportunity like that slip through your fingers, I was going to go full Erica on your ass." They laugh again.

"Speaking of Erica, why didn't she come with us? I thought you said her period never showed."

"It didn't, but she said she didn't want to chance it coming down while she was here. Plus, she's not feeling the best. I think she's dealing with pre-period cramps or something like that."

Chamere nods her head, "Oh, OK… got you. So, what do y'all do when the other one is on? Do y'all come down here solo?"

"I come down here every ladies' night, homegirl or not. I'm getting all my money's worth. Besides, I'm on birth control, so as long as I remember my shot, I won't have to worry about my period crashing my freak party."

"That's smart. I'm sure you don't want nothing standing between you and Stallion's face." Beyonka giggles at Chamere's joke.

"Right, cause girl… that damn beard does something to me!"

"I won't lie… it is sexy as hell."

"Ladies!" The sound of Liyan's voice over the loudspeakers brings an end to Beyonka and Chamere's gossiping. Chamere's vision shoots straight to Liyan's office door without her permission. She looks away after regaining control of herself.

"I know we have a certain way of doing things around here, and for the most part, we stick to the script; but tonight… tonight, we're doing something a little different."

The door opening at the top of the staircase garners every female's attention. Liyan appears, causing every woman in attendance to gasp shockingly. Beyonka's face is covered in disbelief when she grabs Chamere's arm. Chamere is so stunned that she doesn't know what to do.

Liyan stomps down the stairs looking like no one in Club Liquor has ever seen him look before. His utility boots carry him to the bottom step. He lifts the microphone to his mouth, "Tonight, I'm not a businessman, the owner of this club, or even the MC."

His topless body moves towards Chamere, causing her to stiffen like a board. He gazes into her eyes his entire stroll over. The men against the wall walk over to join him. They line up in their usual intimidating way. "Tonight, I'm one of the fellas."

The women lose their shit after Liyan's surprising announcement. The air is suddenly thick with heavy anticipation. Even though the misters' presence demands a high rate of attention, every ounce of feminine energy is being directed towards Liyan.

He's the big fish that no woman has ever been able to catch.

His shirtless body reveals a display of glistening muscles that deserve to be worshipped. His mouthwatering abs disappear inside the top of his ripped jeans like they're playing a game of hide and seek. His fitted cap brings out a thuggish side of him that no one hardly sees.

He engages strongly with Chamere. Her heart is beating so fast that she's afraid it's going to explode. She's so thrown off by Liyan's unorthodox presence that she can't feel Beyonka's constant nudging. Her extreme nervousness is written all over her face. Liyan is loving his effect on her.

"Now fellas… let's see who's on the menu tonight."

CHAPTER SEVEN
One Month Free

The men disperse but Liyan stays put. His eyes are all over Chamere's body. She looks away when the moment becomes too much for her. The other women are gawking at them when Liyan closes in on Chamere.

He cuts his microphone off, "I told you I'd hang up my suit and tie to handle you," he states in a sexy tone. Chamere's mind is racing but she can't get her mouth to verbally express her thoughts. He leans in to whisper in her ear, "So, tell me, Chamere… how do you like to be eaten?" That question coming from him nearly takes her breath away.

She panics, "Liyan, what about the rules?" He looks at her curiously.

"What rules?"

"I don't have on a skirt or dress," she mentions skittishly.

He chuckles to himself after taking in her body again, "And? That's not an official rule. It's more of an unwritten suggestion. Skirts can go up and pants can come down." He plays with the elastic band on the waist of her leggings, "Besides, I'm a hunter and gatherer. I love working for my meal."

Shit!

She swiftly thinks of something else, "But what about the STD test? I have yet to see your clinician." He nods his head slightly as if she has a point.

"True. Usually, ladies with visitor's passes don't participate in our extracurricular activities. It's mainly because they don't want to, but it is really because of protocol."

"Precisely. So why break the protocol for me? Why am I so special?" He stares at her intensely. She breathes away the nervousness that is trying its best to return. His tongue slowly licks the innards of his lips.

"Do you really want me to answer that?"

She takes a deep breath, "I do."

Liyan reaches out his hand for her to grab. She hesitates before taking it, "Follow me, then."

Liyan leads Chamere to the staircase. The other ladies douse her with nasty and envious stares. The jealous women turn their sights to the misters after Liyan removes himself from the playing field. Liyan opens his office door, and they walk inside.

"Should I close it?" Chamere asks anxiously.

"If you want," Liyan replies. She inches the door closed a few seconds later. She turns to face him and his elegant office space. He sets his microphone near other electronic equipment.

She swallows hard, "So…" Liyan glares at her hard like he's studying her. He leans against his large desk situated in the middle of the room.

"So…" he repeats.

She smacks her lips, "Look, Liyan, I'm not good at this type of thing, and I don't like playing games-"

"Who said I was playing a game?"

She sighs. "Liyan, why me?"

He approaches her with a dominant stride, stopping right before their bodies touch. He towers over her, "Honestly, I can't put my finger on why. It's just something about you that makes me want you so fucking bad." Chamere is flattered even though she tries her best to hide it.

She looks up at him. "But who said I wanted you?" she inquires in an unconvincing tone.

Liyan chuckles, "Really?"

She rolls her eyes, "Alright, whatever… scratch that." He chuckles again, "So, because you 'want me bad', you're willing to break the rules of the club?"

Liyan grabs her hand, "Firstly, I made the rules, so I can change or enforce them however I see fit. Secondly…" His hand slides up her arm, causing goosebumps to form all over her skin, "I trust you. That body of yours looks too sweet to be tainted."

"But you don't know me, and you don't know anything about my body." He gestures that he agrees with her.

"You're right, so let me ask you: Do you have a sexually transmitted disease?"

She looks offended, "No!"

He smiles, "Exactly; and as far as what your body wants, I'm sure I can figure that out."

Even though she's secretly enjoying being this close to Liyan, she forces herself to take a step away from him, "My body doesn't want anything from you right now; and when I said that you don't know me, I was referring to me mentally, not physically."

Liyan sighs, "Fine. So, what do you propose we do, then?"

"I know this may be a little hard to wrap your head around, but how about we talk?"

Liyan shakes his head. "I would much rather be doing something else with my mouth, but if talking is what you want to do, then talking is what we'll do."

$$$

"Wow, this thing is pretty thick," Chamere expresses when Liyan slides her a membership contract. He sits on one side of his desk and she on the other. His topless body leans back in his chair.

"That's what she said," he jokes. She rolls her eyes at his terrible sense of humor. "No, but for real, it has to be. You can't imagine the things that could possibly go wrong in a place like this." Chamere nods her head as if she has some idea.

"How much is a membership?"

"$500 a month."

"$500?!" Chamere exclaims in an alarmed tone. Liyan chuckles.

"Yes, $500; but this place is definitely worth it."

She smacks her lips at him while skimming through the pages, "How so? It says here that the misters aren't allowed to kiss or have sexual intercourse with us, so I'm supposed to pay half a rack for what? Some head? You do know how easy head is to get, right?"

"Absolutely, but it's not about the act of getting head, but the quality of the head you're receiving." Liyan's statement intrigues her. He stands to his feet before continuing, "These fellas are the cream of the crop in this area. These are men that most women lust over every time they see them. They are the ones that many ladies know they can't have… except for at a place like this." Chamere's conflicting facial expression lets Liyan know that she's not buying his explanation. He sits near her on the edge of his desk.

"Think about it: You had an awful day at work. You go home to a guy that is barely interested in you, let alone your day. He doesn't give you the attention you deserve or make you feel like the beautiful queen you are. He won't caress you--- touch you--- satisfy your body. He's just… there. So, you come here on Wednesday nights to let your hair down. You are guaranteed to come across a guy that is physically the man of your dreams; and not only is he that, but he talks to you, makes you laugh, wraps his strong arms around you, makes you feel valued. He caters to you, rubs your feet if he has to, fetches you a drink or two if that's what your heart desires; and then, he lays you down and massages your body, making sure not to skip over your neglected clitoris. He guarantees an orgasmic experience, and if you want more, he'll put his face between your legs and fuck you with his tongue… and he won't stop until you cum down his throat. He'll even hold you afterwards."

Chamere fans herself once Liyan's very descriptive scenario makes her hot. Liyan smirks, "And that can happen up to five times a month, so do you still think $500 is too much for an experience like that?"

"So, these women are in relationships, but they're buying companionship?" she inquires, completely dodging Liyan's question. He lets it slide.

"Whether they are or aren't is none of our business. We are not here to question, pry, or judge. We're here to make them feel good, that's all. It doesn't have to be sexual all the time, either. It can be whatever she feels is missing from her personal life. Most of the time, it is sexual, though."

The room falls silent after Liyan's words. He gawks at Chamere as if he's telepathically asking her to give it a try. She breaks their eye contact, "Wow. All of that sounds great and all, but I still don't think this club is for me. Call me old-fashioned, but I prefer real emotional connections over physical or fake ones."

Liyan huffs, "OK. I can respect that." He proceeds to his chair and sits down. He glances at the contract and then at her. He quickly conjures up an idea, "How about I give you your first month free? You can continue to come out with your girls, enjoy the club and get your free drink on. I want you to get a real feel of the place before completely writing it off. Afterwards, if you're still not interested, I'll leave the subject alone for good."

Chamere looks at Liyan as if a cat has her tongue. Chamere has her morals, but what Liyan is offering may be too good of an opportunity to pass on. She takes a deep breath before deciding to entertain Liyan's proposition, "Liyan, are you sure about this?"

"Surer than I've been about anything in a long time."

Chamere blushes, "And you promise to let the subject die if I'm not interested?"

He lifts three fingers, "Scout's honor." Chamere leans back in her chair this time. She thinks hard about his proposal and decides that accepting a free membership wouldn't be so bad.

It's only for a month. What could it hurt?

She leans forward and grabs the contract, "Do you have a pen?"

Liyan smiles devilishly, "Of course I do." He slides one her way. She reads over the last page that requires a signature. She is signing her name shortly thereafter. She pushes the paperwork towards Liyan for him to inspect. He glances at her name on the dotted line, "Chamere Briggs, this is going to be fun." He rubs his hands together, "Now, I need a copy of your ID and after that, I have to call the clinician. It's time to get you tested."

CHAPTER EIGHT
Tested

Chamere stands at the two-way window that overlooks the club below while waiting for the clinician to arrive. One side of Liyan's office watches over the official Club Liquor's dance floor and the other side gives the viewer a front row seat to the hot and steamy actions being exchanged from the misters to the ladies.

Chamere searches for Beyonka in the sea of sexual performances. She spots her on a couch against the wall riding Stallion's face. His hands palm her bare ass cheeks while he repeatedly catches her bouncing pussy with his horse tongue. Sweat trickles down Beyonka's exposed breasts. Stallion's beard shines with the juices of her pleasure.

Beyonka's entire body vibrates when he decides to take the reins. He holds her in place with his strong arms, sucking on her clit like he wants to take it home with him. Beyonka's entire body vibrates when she relinquishes control. She shouts when Stallion's talents make her cum.

Chamere stares at them until her own juices begin to flow. She turns to face Liyan, "So, how did you get involved in something like this anyway?"

He removes his cap to put on a white beater. Chamere is secretly sad to see his amazing chest being covered. He places the fitted hat backwards over his waves, "That's a long story."

"I'm sure you have time to tell it. Your clinician said it will take her about an hour to get here."

He nods his head, "Yeah, you're right. I'm going to need a drink first before I get into all of that, though." He opens the bottom drawer of his desk and produces a bottle of scotch. Two glasses come out next, "Join me?"

Chamere moves in his direction, "That bad, huh?"

He pours two double shots, "Naw. It's just been a long time since I traveled that far down memory lane, but you said you wanted to talk, so…"

He walks around his desk to hand her a glass. She thanks him. They stand closely to each other, "When I was in college, I was a big frat boy. My brothers and I would throw the most epic parties. That's how I learned all about women and their desires." He gently grabs Chamere by the waist to lead her to the window that overlooks the main side of Club Liquor. The vacant space looks like a typical club, equipped with two bars, a DJ booth, a few tables, and a dance floor. He takes a sip from his glass without letting her go.

"After graduation, three of us decided to go into business together: Me, Quan, and O'Ryan. Since we knew what it took to throw a good party, we decided to open a club." Chamere sips from her glass. She loves the sound of Liyan's voice while he holds her. He grins at her like he knows what she's thinking.

"Anyway, we ended up with the name, 'liquor', after realizing that the beginning of our names spelled out the word. We thought the double entendre would be dope for business."

"So, at what point did it become a triple entendre? From 'liquor' to 'lick-her'?" Liyan chuckles.

"I'm impressed that you picked up on that; most people don't." He points towards the empty nightclub, "What you are looking at is the original Club Liquor. This was the first of our three locations. Each one of us runs one now. When we first opened, business was OK. It definitely wasn't nothing to hoot and holler about. It wasn't until I overheard a few ladies talking that I got the 'ladies' night' idea. They kept saying how they wished a place existed where they could go and be worshipped by fine men. I knew they were joking, but they were still on to something. After about a year of legal stuff, recruiting the right fellas, and preparing an erotic enough space, ladies' night was officially born."

Liyan leads Chamere to the other window. The raunchy live-action show makes Chamere blush. She fights the sexual tension that is steadily growing between her and Liyan. He clears his throat when the pornographic activities begin getting to him as well.

"To say my idea was a hit is an understatement. We were at capacity every Wednesday night, even turning away ladies because we didn't have the means to cater to them. That's when the guys and I figured it was best to open another location. Eventually, two turned into three and we're looking to open a fourth club as we speak."

Chamere looks impressed, even though she still doesn't fully agree with the details of "ladies' night". She turns to face him, "Congratulations. It sounds like things are really working out for you."

He tugs her closer to him, engaging with her in a way he hasn't done with anyone in a long time. She looks surprised, "Thanks. I guess things are going OK. I'm not going to be ungrateful and complain, because business speaking, I'm successful as fuck; but this business shit has put a real damper on my personal life. I can't remember the last time I kicked it with a woman like this."

"That's because all we've been to you lately is moments of pleasure and dollar signs."

He wants to disagree with her, but he quickly realizes he can't. "You may have a point."

They stare at each other for no real reason at all. The room gets heavy with lustful desire. Liyan's hand massages the small of Chamere's back. She nibbles on her bottom lip, causing him to lick his. Chamere feels his dick growing against her pelvis.

KNOCK! KNOCK!

The sound of someone knocking at the door extinguishes the fire that was starting between the two. Liyan releases Chamere, "Come in."

"Hey, handsome," the woman dressed in scrubs blurts out as soon as she enters the room. She appears a little shocked to see Liyan standing so closely to Chamere.

"Hey, Sharee," Liyan says back. Sharee hesitates before throwing her hand up in greeting. Liyan continues, "This is Chamere, Club Liquor's newest member. She needs the introductory exam. Take care of her for me."

$$$

"So… I saw you go inside the examination room with the clinician last night. Is it safe to say that you are now the proud owner of a ladies' night membership?" Beyonka asks Chamere over breakfast. Erica nearly spits out her oatmeal at the news.

Chamere grins, "I'm surprised you saw anything besides the wall you were facing while you were grinding on Stallion's face."

Beyonka blushes, "Girl… don't even get me started on Stallion! That man knows my body too well."

Chamere laughs, "You don't have to tell me; I was there. I saw it all." Erica smacks her lips as if that was a diss towards her.

"And don't try to change the subject! What made you change your mind about getting a membership? Was it Liyan's head skills that convinced you?" Beyonka smiles nosily.

"Liyan's head skills? OK, what did I miss?" Erica blurts out shockingly.

"Mr. Club Owner himself decided he was a mister last night, and I'm sure it was because Chamere was there."

Erica's mouth hangs open, "What!"

Beyonka nods her head, "Yes, girl. You should have seen him: Tim boots, Trues, fitted hat, oily chest, and all. I mean, could you imagine Liyan out of a suit?" Erica shakes her head no. Beyonka continues, "Anyway, from the moment he stepped onto the main floor, his eyes were set on Chamere. He wouldn't even look in the direction of another chick. It was something to see." Erica's eyes are bigger than Chamere has ever seen them.

Chamere smirks at her reaction, "Yeah… to say I was flattered is an understatement. I was definitely not expecting that."

"What else weren't you expecting? How good his tongue game was, perhaps?" Beyonka pries devilishly.

"And where did you get the funds for a membership? You don't make that kind of money," Erica interrupts nastily. Chamere rolls her eyes at her.

"It wasn't like that, Beyonka. When he took me up to his office, all we did was talk. He told me about his life and how he and his frat brothers started Club Liquor. He is so fun to kick it with." She turns to address Erica, "And I didn't have to come up with any kind of money because my membership was free. Liyan insisted."

Beyonka and Erica pause all movements as if the surprise from Chamere's confession has paralyzed them. Beyonka drops her fork, "I'm sorry… did you say 'free'?"

Chamere nods her head while chewing, "Yeah. Liyan gave me the first month free. He wants me to give the place a try before I make a final decision." The room gets uncomfortably quiet all of a sudden. Chamere looks confused, "What? Is something wrong?"

"I mean… I'm just wowed, that's all. Free? I don't think I've ever heard of him giving away a free membership before. Have you, Erica?"

"Hell no… and honestly, I think that's interesting." She glares at Chamere, "Just last week, you were ready to boycott the damn place for lack of morality. Now, you're under a contract that you swore you would never sign in a million years. Who knew that a million years would pass by so quickly?"

CHAPTER NINE
Best Friends

"Ever since then, they've been acting weird towards me. We haven't said two words to each other all day. Even Beyonka is keeping her distance from me," Chamere says frustratedly. She has one ear against her pillow and the other against her cellphone.

Liyan responds, "That's how it goes. There are two topics that will always come between friendships: Pleasure and money. Limiting the talk about both helps cut down on a lot of confusion."

"Yeah, but Beyonka, too, though? I expect shit from Erica, but not Beyonka. I really thought Beyonka was my friend." Chamere sighs, "I guess it is what it is. I should have kept the membership shit to myself." The heavy topic causes a moment of silence to linger. Chamere closes her eyes.

"What are you doing right now?" Liyan asks.

"Nothing. Laying here talking to you."

"Well, let me make you feel better. How about we continue this conversation over dinner. My treat…"

Chamere's eyes pop open, "Like a date?"

Liyan chuckles, "Naw. Like two people that enjoy talking to each other doing so while eating."

Chamere shakes her head, "Now that you put it that way, it sounds irresistible." They both laugh.

"Shoot me your address. I'll be there in an hour."

After sending Liyan the details he requested, Chamere paces her floor with anxiousness. "He said it's not a date…" she keeps reminding herself. She glances at her favorite pair of jeans, "But he could just be saying that to be sarcastic."

She stares at the handful of dresses in her closet. She frowns at the thought of wearing one of them. She hates how uncomfortable dresses are, and even worse, how sexually suggestive they are.

"But you'll be with Liyan," she whispers. She grins when her thoughts flashback to his perfect smile and amazing physique. She reaches for the skimpiest one she owns, which still boasts its price tag. She sighs, "Extreme circumstances call for extreme measures." She holds it against her body while staring in the mirror, "Here goes nothing."

$$$

"Damn, Chamere. You looking good, girl," Liyan compliments when she walks out of the house. He gawks at her as if she is the planned dessert after dinner. Even though he looks great, his black jeans and fitted tee make her feel slightly overdressed. He holds the passenger door open for her to enter the car.

"Why, thank you, Liyan," Chamere states sweetly. He gets in a few moments later. "Wow, this is a nice piece of machinery," she points out while checking out his ride.

Liyan pulls off before responding, "Thanks. I'm thinking about parking it and getting something newer. I'm getting a little tired of it."

"Must be nice. I'm still standing at the bus stop."

Liyan glances in her direction, "Circumstances like that don't last always, especially when you have a hustler spirit. All it takes is the right opportunity, or person, to change things for you forever." Liyan glances at Chamere with serious eyes. She's not sure if he's hinting towards something or not, but she's very interested in finding out.

"Where are we headed?" She questions while staring out of the window.

"I have a little business to handle, and I was hoping you wouldn't mind handling it with me. I was going to hit up my chef friend to see if she could hook us up something special while we get some work done."

"Work?" She glances at the small dress she's wearing, instantly regretting her decision to wear it. "You should have told me we were doing work. I'm not dressed to do anything work-related."

Liyan glares at her bare thighs and licks his lips, "Shid, that body is working me right now." Chamere smacks her lips and Liyan smiles, "I'm just playing; but don't worry, it's not that type of work… not for you anyway. Mainly, I want you to be by my side while I get shit done. Is that OK with you?" Chamere nods her head that it is. "Cool. We're almost there."

Liyan and Chamere pull up at Club Liquor a short time later. They exit his car. "Club Liquor… of course," Chamere mumbles disappointedly.

Liyan grabs her hand and leads her towards the front door, "Is that a hint of disgust I hear?"

She smiles, "No, I just thought we were going somewhere else, that's all."

He unlocks the club and flicks the switches once they get inside. He locks the door behind them. "I'm sorry to disappoint you, then, gorgeous. Next time we hit the streets, I promise to let you choose our destination."

"Mm-hmm," she replies facetiously. She explores the official side of Club Liquor for the first time. It looks a lot better up close but it's still an ordinary nightclub.

"So… what do you think?" Liyan heads behind the bar to pour them a drink. Chamere stands in the middle of the dance floor.

"I think it's a club." Liyan smacks his lips. "I'm sorry, Liyan, but I'm not a party girl. I mean, I went out a few times when I turned 21, but now, I'm over it."

He signals for her to join him. He hands her a glass, "Damn, Chamere. How are we supposed to be best friends if you don't like clubs?"

She giggles, "Best friends?"

He nods his head, "Yeah. I know we're not doing all of this talking for no reason. You know more about me than most people."

She blushes, "Oh, is that so?" He smiles this time, "And I don't have to like clubs for us to be best friends, I just have to respect what you do."

Liyan moves closer to her, "So, you respect what I do?"

Chamere gestures that she's on the fence about it. "The jury is still out on that one." They grin. "What are we doing here, anyway? Aren't you about to open soon?"

"Nope. I don't open on Thursdays or Mondays. I reserve Thursdays for paperwork and club maintenance. Mondays are for disinfection and meeting with the fellas."

"Oh… you mean, the misters," Chamere moans out sarcastically.

Liyan smiles, "Yes, the misters, as you ladies call them." They sip from their glasses. "Today, I have a little paperwork to do, but I mainly need to fix a few tables and chairs that some customers complained were wobbly. The chef will be here soon to make us a steak dinner. You do like steak, don't you?"

"Of course I do. I didn't get these thighs by skipping out on red meat." The mention of Chamere's legs put them on Liyan's radar again. He bites his bottom lip.

"They look so smooth and soft... I would love to touch them. Will I ever get that chance?"

Chamere blushes, "That's such a weird question. Am I supposed to say, 'yes' to that?"

"You can say whatever you want, but I'm hoping you say yes." Chamere makes an unsure face. He pulls her into him, "Would it had been better if I just grabbed them instead of asking?"

"Um… I don't know. It surely would've been less awkward, that's for sure."

"I thought you wanted me to be a gentleman…"

She gazes into his eyes, "You're touching me right now without my permission but I'm not objecting."

Her voice is flirtatious and filled with suggestion. Liyan smirks as if he has been challenged. "Mental note taken. Don't worry, sexy… I got you."

CHAPTER TEN
Chef Keisha

Chamere sits at the bar sipping her drink while Liyan works on leveling a table. He removes his shirt when the manual labor becomes too heated for his already hot physique.

"Fuck…" Chamere mumbles under her breath. Liyan has a body that was shaped by God Almighty himself. He stands to his feet to check the results of his work. He lifts the table effortlessly with one hand and turns it upright. The sweat rolling down his hills of chest muscles makes Chamere nibble on her bottom lip.

Liyan notices her lustful eyes, "See something you like?"

She blushes, "Oh, be quiet. You already know how fine you are. I don't have to tell you that."

He smirks sexily while moving in her direction, "I didn't know that you thought I was fine. What else do you think about me?"

He removes his work gloves and sets them on a bar stool. He grabs his glass from the bar and takes a gulp. She rolls her eyes, "I think that you are cocky as hell, and of course, full of yourself." Liyan looks offended. Chamere giggles.

"Oh, really? Cocky and full of myself, huh?" He sets his drink down before standing in front of Chamere. She bites her finger at the sight of the perspiration running down his tight abs. He rubs his hands down both of her legs and parts them strongly, taking her by surprise.

"Liyan, what are you-" He slides his body between her thighs before she's able to finish her inquiry. He grabs her ass and slides her pelvis towards his. The bottom of her dress rolls up to her waist. Her thin panty is the only thing standing between Liyan and her vagina.

The bulge in his jeans rests perfectly against Chamere's awakening clit. He rolls his hips in circular motions to stimulate her spot. Her legs react favorably to his actions.

"If you're going to call me full of myself, then the least I can do is earn it. Is this what you meant by cocky? Can you feel my cockiness now?" Chamere has no interest in answering Liyan's questions. She can't take her mind off of how great Liyan's dick print feels between her covered pussy lips.

"I think she likes me," Liyan whispers about Chamere's moistening vagina. The seat of her underwear becomes covered in her love nectar. She closes her eyes when her feelings of ecstasy grow with every passing second. Liyan watches Chamere's facial expressions attentively, allowing her bliss to dictate his movements. His dick hardens more, intensifying the pressure on her clitoris.

"Shit, Liyan. Why are you so good at this?" She moans out.

He places his mouth close to her ear, "If you think this is something, just wait until you feel my tongue. I can eat you so good right now that you'll be shouting my name. You can cum in my mouth as many times as your body can handle… my tongue never gets tired. Why are you playing with me, Chamere?"

She throws her arms around his neck once her pelvis unwillingly grinds to the rhythm of Liyan's movements. She had no idea that dry humping could be this pleasing. Her body shivers harder.

"Why get tested if you're not going to let me taste you?" She ignores him again. The perfect pressure that Liyan is applying to her clit is enough to make any woman speechless. He speeds up when her breathing becomes broken. She holds him tightly when she nears an orgasm.

KNOCK! KNOCK!

The sound of the chef's arrival startles them both. Chamere shivers violently as soon as Liyan stops. She frowns, "Dammit, Liyan! Come on, just a few seconds longer." Her voice is filled with eagerness and frustration. Liyan takes a step away from her. He eases her soaked panty to the side and slides his middle finger between her pussy lips. She flinches when he brushes past her swollen clit. He sucks her flavor from his finger.

"So fucking sweet… just like I thought." He smirks while taking a few steps backwards. He turns to head towards the club door. The disappointment covering Chamere's face is blatant. He glances over his shoulder, "Don't worry… we'll finish this later. I promise."

$$$

"Hey, Liyan, with your sexy ass. Damn, no shirt?" the woman asks as soon as he opens the door. She hugs him tightly, followed by a kiss on his cheek. Chamere is slightly taken aback by the chef's over-friendly greeting. She tugs her dress down.

"Keish, I want you to meet my new friend, Chamere. Chamere, this is Keisha; one of the best cooks in the state." Keisha looks thrown off by Chamere's presence at the bar. Chamere stands awkwardly, trying her best to overcome the clitoral stimulation she just received.

"It's nice to meet you," Chamere states, approaching the chef with an extended hand. Keisha reluctantly shakes it.

"Liyan, when you said I would be cooking for you and a friend, I thought you meant either Quan or O'Ryan. I didn't think you meant-"

"Will that be a problem?" Liyan's questions in a stern voice.

Keisha checks herself, "Uh, no… of course not. It's no problem at all." A fake smile covers her face, "My apologies, Mr. Russell. I'll get started right away."

She gives Chamere a nasty look on the way past her. Chamere looks confused, "She's not too friendly, is she?" Liyan doesn't respond. Chamere becomes irritated, "Either y'all used to date, or she really needs to learn how interact with people."

Liyan ignores her insinuations, "Well, she wasn't asked here to display her social skills, only her cooking ones." His dismissive response catches Chamere off guard. He glances in her direction, "I need to work on the rest of these tables and chairs. I want to be finished by the time dinner is ready. Help yourself to as many drinks as you'd like. I'll try to be quick."

Chamere's eyes follow him as he walks away from her. She places her hands on her hips.

What the hell was that about?

CHAPTER ELEVEN
Liyan Hearted

The drinks are constantly flowing, even though Chamere is mostly drinking alone. Liyan takes a sip from his glass every once in a while, but every time he approaches the bar to get it, he barely looks at Chamere. It's apparent that Liyan is acting differently now that Keisha is around.

She's officially ready to go home.

Chamere is more buzzed than she's been in a while. The liquor does nothing to help with the uncomfortable situation she's in. She's feeling some type of way by the time their steaks are ready. She relocates to the table where Keisha is setting their plates.

"If you need anything else, I'll be in the kitchen," Keisha snarls in Liyan's direction. He never replies to her statement, angering her even more. She stomps away as quickly as she can. Liyan joins Chamere, "Looks good, doesn't it?"

Chamere gawks at Liyan, allowing the alcohol to make her more emotional than usual. She's jealous of Keisha and she's not sure why. She stands up from the table before she says something she will regret, "Excuse me."

"What are you doing, Chamere?" she asks herself as soon as she steps inside of the bathroom. She stares at her reflection like she hardly recognizes herself. The sound of the toilet flushing startles her. She spins around to face Keisha as she emerges from the middle stall.

"I'm sure you're doing what the rest of us have done; allowing Liyan to sweet talk his way into your panties, and then your heart," Keisha states while heading to the sink to wash her hands. She successfully ignores Chamere's gawking.

Chamere is beyond confused, "Excuse me? What did you just say?"

"You heard exactly what I said, new girl." She turns to face Chamere like she has a problem with her. Chamere gets on defense, allowing her liquored state to make her more confrontational than usual. Keisha backs off once she notices how hostile the environment is getting, "Look, I'm not trying to start shit with you. I was the new girl once upon a time, so I get it. That's the thing, though; there will always be a new girl. Right now, it's you. By the end of the month, it'll be someone else."

Chamere doesn't want to entertain Keisha's claims, but she can't help but to entertain something that sounds so valid. She bites, "So, he does this shit often? Like, sweet talk women into falling for him?" Keisha nods her head yes. Chamere grinds her teeth, "Who has fallen for it?"

"Shit--- everyone. Me, his clinician, a few other women I know..."

"Well, how does he usually do it?" Chamere needs to know. She's hoping that Liyan is not running the same game on her that he did on them.

Keisha folds her arms, "You don't want to believe me, do you?" She shakes her head, "You were a visitor for ladies' night, right? You were reluctant at first… didn't buy into this whole 'pay to pamper' bullshit. He singled you out; made you feel special; tried to talk you into signing a contract." The look covering Chamere's face lets Keisha know that she is spot on. She continues, "Seeing as how he's still spending time with you, y'all must have just started hanging out. Has he ate your pussy yet?"

Chamere is alarmed by the blunt, but accurate question, "No, but he keeps trying to."

Keisha smirks, "That's how he gets you hooked. Liyan eats pussy like he's in love with you, and he will keep eating it until you fall in love with him. Then, he'll have you right where he wants you."

"Which is where?" Chamere asks fearfully.

"In the palm of his hands, which looks different for everyone. With his clinician, he uses her to run the STD screenings and physical exams. For me, I became the head of the kitchen. I oversee the food for the club… and the list goes on and on."

Chamere's feelings are visibly hurt. Keisha starts to feel bad for her, "Look, I know this is hard to hear, but it's the truth. This is all a game to Liyan; an extension of this bullshit club he loves so much. He operates the same way personally: No kissing, no sex, no emotional attachments. If he met you in the club, then he will always interact with you according to his club's rules."

"So why deal with him after finding all of this out? You are still working for him and so is the clinician," Chamere points out.

Keisha makes an embarrassed face, "That's true, and I wish I had an answer for that. The money is good, but I'd be lying if I said that's the only reason why I stay. He's just so fine… and smart… and he's attentive when he wants to be… and he knows how to satisfy a woman. He's so hard to walk away from once you've experienced all of that."

Chamere is defeated. She knew that Liyan was too good to be true, but she entertained him anyway. She walks towards the exit as if she can't stomach anymore stories from one of Liyan's previous conquests.

Keisha stops her, "I did try to leave once. I was tired of his games. I was prepared to let him go but he knew exactly what to do to make me stay. He knows exactly what to do to make all of us stay."

$$$

"Can you please stop and tell me what I did?" Liyan asks a stewing Chamere. After her powwow with Keisha in the ladies' room, she demanded that Liyan take her home. She never touched her steak, and he barely took a bite of his. He asked Keisha to wrap them up to go.

"Nothing. You didn't do anything," Chamere answers in the most unbelievable tone Liyan has ever heard. She gets in his car and faces the passenger window. He stares at her after getting in.

"I was hoping we could go for a ride after dinner-"

"I said I want to go home," Chamere spits out without looking his way.

He expels a loud breath, "Fine."

Liyan pulls off a minute later. They ride in awkward silence. The animosity in the air is killing him. Liyan pulls over on the dark shoulder without warning, catching Chamere off guard. Her anger grows, "I said I want to go home! I swear to God, Liyan, I'll walk-"

"Chamere, would you calm down!" He cuts her off to shout. She glances in his direction. He turns to engage with her, "Now please… tell me what the fuck is going on? What happened that got you so upset?"

"I don't know… maybe you should ask Keisha!" Chamere yells before she realizes it. She feels completely unstable the moment her words leave her mouth.

Liyan's nostrils flare, "What the fuck did she say to you?"

Chamere calms down. "Nothing that I didn't already know."

Liyan looks taken aback, "What is that supposed to mean?"

"It means that I don't think it's a good idea for us to see each other anymore."

Liyan quickly grabs her hand, "Whoa… wait a minute. Where is all of this coming from?"

"What is it that you want from me, Liyan?" He appears confused by her question. She attempts to clarify, "I mean, why are you doing all of this? Why are you inviting me out on 'non-dates'? Why are you saying we're going to be best friends when you know it's not true?"

"Why would I lie about something like that? Of course it's true."

"So, in your world, best friends exchange sexual favors? They flirt like we do with each other? They fucking dry hump in empty clubs?" Liyan is stumped by the line of questioning. She continues, "Just how many best friends do you have?" Liyan is speechless. His silence speaks volumes to Chamere. She sighs, "Liyan, just take me home."

She unplugs from their conversation once and for all. Her attention goes back to the passenger side window. Liyan stares at her for a few seconds with a strong desire to explain. He decides to drive off instead. Liyan drops Chamere off with no further words exchanged. He pulls off before she makes it to the front door.

CHAPTER TWELVE
Two Can Play that Game

"I wish I would have never entertained his ass. I was really starting to like him, too. Ugh! How could I have been so stupid?" Chamere exclaims to Beyonka.

Beyonka sighs, "Well, at least you found out who he really was before you were intimate with him. Damn, I can't believe he has been going around warping bitches' minds with tongue control! It can't possibly be that good."

Beyonka makes Chamere grin, which she hasn't done in nearly a week. Beyonka looks accomplished, "There you go. I haven't seen your smile in so long that I forgot what it looked like."

Erica walks into Beyonka's room to join the chatting ladies. They are surprised to see her in club gear. Erica pauses when she notices their eyes on her, "What?"

"So, you're going this week?" Beyonka inquires.

Erica checks herself out in the mirror, "Yeah. I might as well."

"But I thought you were feeling crappy?" Chamere adds.

Erica fixes her tiny skirt, "I was, but I think it passed."

"And what about your period? Did it finally show?"

"I'm not worried about my period, and neither should you. I think it's changing course or something. It's no big deal." Chamere watches her roommates primp for ladies' night while she sits on Beyonka's bed wearing sweatpants and a t-shirt. She doesn't plan on visiting Club Liquor again for as long as she lives.

Erica hesitates awkwardly before turning to address Chamere, "Look, I'm sorry about you and Liyan, but you can't let what he did ground you. Fuck him! If he can play games, then so can you."

Erica visits Beyonka's closet and pulls out the slutty dress Beyonka was going to let Chamere borrow for her first ladies' night. Beyonka's eyes grow wide with approval. Erica walks it over to Chamere after admiring it. "Here, put this on. You're coming with us tonight."

Chamere shakes her head, "I can't. I don't think I'm ready to face Liyan yet."

Erica flops down next to Chamere, "So don't. Don't face him at all. This isn't about him, Chamere, it's about you. You qualify to participate in the ladies' night festivities this week, so I think you should participate. Find you a handsome face to stick between your legs. If you want to get over Liyan, then the best way to do it is by getting under someone else."

$$\$\$\$$$

Chamere makes a nervous face when she approaches Club Liquor's back door. Anxiety engulfs her as soon as she flashes her brand-new gold card at Big Bubba, "I don't know about this, y'all."

She tugs at the microscopic material that is supposed to be the bottom of her outfit. Her ass cheeks jiggle from underneath her dress every time she takes a step. Beyonka giggles, "Girl, just leave it alone. In about 30 minutes, everyone will see you naked anyway."

Chamere panics at the possibility of the entire club seeing her nude. The thought alone makes her want to turn around and head straight home. Beyonka reads the alarmed expression on her face, "It's no big deal. Erica and I get undressed all of the time. All of the women here do, as a matter of fact. You know that; you've seen it with your own two eyes."

"Ladies! You know what time it is!" Liyan announces from over the loudspeakers. Chamere rolls her eyes as soon as she hears his voice. She chooses to tune him out for the rest of his bullshit intro. She stares at the misters uninterestedly as they approach the women.

"See someone worth face-fucking?" Beyonka whispers to Chamere jokingly. Chamere displays a fake smile as a way to pacify Beyonka. The truth is, she is nowhere near in the mood to be sexually involved with any of the misters, especially since each one of them have probably licked every vagina in attendance.

No, thanks.

"There goes Dino," Beyonka mutters to Erica. Dino glares at Erica as if she's the only woman in the club. Erica acts like she doesn't notice, even though it's apparent she does. He approaches the group.

"Hello, ladies," Dino greets them with a smile. His dimples are always a pleasure to see.

"Hello, Dino," everyone responds but Erica. Beyonka and Chamere stare at her weirdly.

Dino steps closer to her, "I've been calling and texting you, but you won't hit me back. What's going on?" Erica looks embarrassed after Beyonka and Chamere overhear Dino's concerns. She grabs his arm and pulls him to a quiet corner.

"I wonder what that was about," Beyonka blurts out curiously. "Since when has Dino and Beyonka become phone buddies?"

Chamere humps her shoulders, "I guess nothing is as cut and dry as it's supposed to be at Club Liquor. Having repeated sexual encounters is bound to have some emotional repercussions." Chamere and Beyonka spot Stallion gazing at them. Chamere gestures in his direction, "Exhibit A."

Beyonka giggles. "Oh, hush! It's strictly business between Stallion and me," she lies. She turns to address Chamere quickly, "But look, I don't want to be 'that girl' that leaves her friend when she is going through a crisis, but I really want to get a session in with Stallion before someone else snatches him up. I prefer to be the first pussy he eats. Even though he washes his beard, it's still… well, you know."

Chamere balls her face up at the graphic description. She shoves her friend towards Stallion, "By all means, have fun. I'll be fine."

Chamere approaches the bar as soon as Beyonka disappears with her cowboy-hatted plaything. She sighs her way into a bar stool, "Scotch straight up, please." The bartender pours her a shot, "And keep 'em coming." She swallows the liquor right after her words. She waits patiently for another.

"Liyan… I'm serious. Why do you keep doing this to me?" Chamere overhears the clinician ask in a stressed tone. Chamere glances in the direction of the examination room. Her eyes grow wide when she spots Liyan's arm wrapped around the clinician's waist. He's whispering something in her ear that calms her down instantly. He appears to be doing exactly what Keisha tried to warn Chamere about. Chamere becomes furious all over again.

"Fuck that arrogant son-of-a-bitch," she mumbles before downing another shot. She grabs the first mister that walks her way. He looks surprised by her aggressive gesture but smiles once he realizes how pretty she is.

"You must be new," he states flirtatiously. She freezes after noticing that he's much more handsome than she initially thought. His gorgeousness delays her reply for a second, "Yes, I am… sort of." She giggles artificially, "I was hoping you could explain to me what a girl has to do to have a good time around here." She takes another shot to give her the courage she needs to keep up this charade.

"Absolutely. You came to the right person, sweetheart. Around here, they call me Showtime. It's so nice to meet your beautiful ass."

She sticks out her hand for him to shake, but he kisses it instead. She blushes, "I'm Chamere.

CHAPTER THIRTEEN
Showtime

Out of all the men in the club (*outside of Liyan*), Showtime is probably the closest to Chamere's type. She stares at his gorgeous, tattooed body while taking in his thuggish nature. He tells her what ladies' night has to offer while she pretends that she has no idea what he's talking about. His perfect smile wraps up his story, "I hope I didn't bore you too much with the textbook shit."

"Not at all," Chamere assures him with a grin. He licks his lips sexily.

"So, what you're trying to tell me is that no one around here has pleased your lovely body yet?" Liyan flashes before Chamere's eyes, but she shakes the thought of him away expeditiously.

"No, and I won't lie… I'm a little nervous about it. I'm not 100% sure I'm comfortable with letting a guy that just licked another woman's vagina lick mine right after that."

Showtime chuckles, "Well, you're in luck because I ain't ate pussy in months. This is actually my first night at the club in a while. I had to leave the state for a few to handle some business. I've been dying to get back so that I can suck the soul out of a woman, though. I missed that shit."

Chamere looks surprised, but slightly intrigued, "But I still don't know you, Showtime. How am I supposed to be comfortable letting you between my legs when I don't know anything about you?"

"That sounds like a problem we can easily fix." Showtime takes her hand and guides her to a couch near the stairs leading to Liyan's office. Chamere sits down while Showtime rests on his knees in front of her. Chamere glares at his handsome face nervously.

He rubs his hands up her smooth legs, "I'm going to tell you whatever it is you desire to know about me. Ask me whatever you want, and I promise, I'll answer. In return, I get to do one thing that I want to do to your sexy ass body." Chamere swallows hard. Her eyes swiftly shift around the pleasure-filled room. Women are being licked as far as the eye can see. Showtime notices her hesitation, "Come on, don't be shy."

He kisses the front of her thighs softly, causing her body to tingle. She forces herself to participate when her sights stumble upon Liyan's office window.

She hopes he's getting an eyeful.

"Well, obviously, I would like to know your name."

Showtime smiles, "Oh, really? That's an easy one." He parts her legs gently with his amazing arms, "My name is Curtis." He admires her edible-looking vagina through her thong with lustful eyes. His patience dwindles once his mouth begins to water. He glances at Chamere, "Keep going. Don't stop now."

His hands sliding towards her private area makes her tense. She goes against her better judgment, "Are you from here?"

He slides her body towards him to remove her panty. He lays the black undergarments next to her, "No, I was born and raised in New Orleans. I didn't move here until my senior year in high school."

He licks his fingers before rubbing them across Chamere's exposed clit. He spreads her leg wide, "Wait! I haven't asked you another question yet."

He lowers his head towards her crotch, "Well, you better hurry up because I'm not stopping. The smell of you has me hungry as fuck. I need to eat you now."

$$$

The sweat covering Chamere's forehead doesn't account for 1% of her body's moisture right now. Her pussy is dripping more than it has ever dripped in her lifetime. Showtime continues catering to her clit, humming on it with vibrating lips. Her legs shiver violently.

She's about to cum already.

"Fuck! Umm, how long have you been doing this?" She questions to buy herself some time. Showtime removes her clit from his wet lips. His glistening face emerges from between her legs. He licks her flavor from around his mouth.

"How long have I been eating pussy or how long have I been working at the club?"

"Both," she responds quickly. Showtime smirks as if he knows what she's trying to do. He massages her clitoris with his thumb to keep her stimulated.

"Well, I started eating pussy at a really young age… my first year in high school maybe; and I started working at the club as soon as ladies' night was created. My frat brothers recruited me. They own the joint."

Chamere's eyes grow three times their normal size after Showtime's words.

He's Liyan's frat brother? Shit!

Showtime ignores Chamere's reaction and goes back to work. The tip of his tongue greets Chamere's hard clitoris. He flicks it slowly before taking it in his mouth. Chamere's legs shake like crazy.

She's about to cum again.

"Shit, Showtime! What's your favorite food?" she asks randomly.

He laughs, "Now, you're reaching. You tell me: What do you think my favorite thing to eat is?" He gives her pussy a long lick before she's able to reply. He purposely slurps every crevice of her. He looks into her eyes, "You know you taste fucking amazing, right? I could literally suck your pussy all day and night."

Chamere blushes, "You are so nasty."

He grins, "Yeah, but I can tell you like it." She neither confirms nor denies his claims. He drapes her legs over his broad shoulders, "Now, are you finally going to stop cock-blocking yourself and let me make you orgasm? I'm trying to see what your cum tastes like."

"O-OK," Chamere mumbles nervously. Showtime repositions himself to prepare for his grand finale. He holds her tightly, sliding his curved tongue inside of her pink opening. Her body spasms with delight.

"Oh my gosh!" She squeals in amazement. Showtime tongue fucks her with a sensual rhythm. She grips the back of his head and closes her eyes when he hits her G-spot. She can't believe how well he's orally penetrating her.

"Mm-hm," Showtime moans with impeccable tongue strokes. Chamere bears down to cum.

"Uhh!" She forces out when her liquid pleasure erupts from her body. Showtime attacks her clit while her squirt trickles down his strong chest. He laps at her clitoris until another orgasm arises. She cums again, convulsing so hard that her body locks up.

"Hell yeah… that's what I like to see," Showtime expresses with a lick of his lips. He releases her after her set of climaxes are complete. Chamere's body twitches uncontrollably when Showtime rises from the floor. He stands over her dominantly like a great conqueror.

He glances at her cum running down his torso, "You got me good, didn't you?"

She makes an unpleasant face once she realizes what he's referring to, "Oh shit! I'm so sorry, Showtime! I had no idea I was a squirter-"

"Don't worry about it, sweetheart. I love bathing in your juices. I'm glad to have been the one to bring 'em out of you."

"Showtime, you do remember the rule about squirting, don't you?" Liyan asks tackily from the bottom step. At some point during Chamere and Showtime's steamy interaction, Liyan crept downstairs with an envious stride. He gawks at Chamere even though he's talking to Showtime. Chamere straightens up and covers herself as if she's been caught doing something she had no business doing.

Showtime makes a weird face, "Uh, is this really the right time to be talking about something like that?"

Liyan finally looks Showtime's way, "Well, you've been gone for a while, so I wanted to make sure you remembered the rules."

"Of course I do," Showtime growls in an irritated tone. Liyan stares him up and down but doesn't say anything further.

Showtime helps Chamere up from the couch. She grabs her panty and stuffs it in her small purse. She successfully ignores Liyan's glares as she turns to face Showtime, "It was so nice to meet you, Chamere. Being your first time was my pleasure. Please don't let it be our last."

He kisses her softly on the cheek before they separate. He shoots Liyan a nasty look on the way past him. Chamere turns to walk away, but Liyan grabs her arm. He spins her around to face him. "I need to see you in my office… now."

CHAPTER FOURTEEN
Playing Games

"What, Liyan?" Chamere spits out as soon as they cross the threshold to his office. Liyan slams the door behind him.

"What the fuck was that about?"

"What was what about?" She plays stupid.

Liyan tightens his jaw, "I thought you weren't interested in participating in ladies' night?"

She folds her arms, "I wasn't, but I am now."

He rubs his waves with his hand before unbuttoning his suit jacket. He sits on the edge of his desk frustratedly, "Why do you keep playing with me, Chamere?"

"I have no idea what you're talking about."

His patience dissipates right before her eyes, "I've been trying to eat you for weeks and you protested repeatedly."

She humps her shoulders, "Yeah…so?"

"So, you let Showtime taste you just like that?" He snaps his fingers when he says "that". She stares at him with no attempts made to answer his question. He stands up angrily, "First, you write me off and tell me you don't want to see me again. Then, you show up to my club and get tongue fucked in front of my office stairs so that I could see. Again, why do you keep playing with me, girl?"

She laughs obnoxiously, "Why do I keep playing with you? Oh, so I guess it's OK for you to play with people but not OK for them to do the same thing to you, huh?"

"What the fuck are you talking about?"

Chamere's anger grows this time. She storms towards him, "Keisha is 'what' I'm talking about! So is your clinician… you think I don't know about your relationships with them?"

"Relationships with them? I don't have a relationship with anyone."

"Do they know that?"

"Of course they do! I'm very clear about my capabilities, expectations, and boundaries."

"Did you relay that information to them before or after you went down on them?" Liyan looks thrown off by the question, "Because I don't remember us discussing any of that, but you surely were adamant about us being intimate!"

Liyan enters her personal space, "I've never forced anything on anyone. They wanted me to eat their pussy, so I ate it. They busted a great nut and got a good paying job, so what's the fucking problem?"

"You know what, Liyan? There is no problem. Continue playing your games with women who show a little resistance when it comes to joining your bullshit club.

That's what you do, right? Try to persuade us to sign on the dotted line by promising us your friendship? By licking us so good that we can no longer think straight?"

"Whoa, now that's crazy. Women turn down access to my club all of the time. You actually think I'm going around eating pussy just to get them to start a membership? Fuck no!" He makes a disgusted face.

Chamere appears skeptical, "So, what is it then? Why did you pick us… me? Why are we so special?"

"First of all, stop grouping y'all together like this is some sort of conspiracy or some shit. I like women for different reasons, just like any man does. I liked Sharee because she's nice and caring. I liked Keisha because she's fun and cool to hang around; and I liked you because…" He steps closer to her, "Because there is something about your soul that makes you seem so familiar to me. Something I was so curious about."

Liyan glares into Chamere's eyes so deeply that it catches her off guard. She swallows hard, "And did you find out what it was that made me seem so familiar?"

He places his palm on the side of her face to engage with her better. Her lips tingle at the thought of him kissing them, "I was working on that, but you cut me off before I could figure it out." His arm wraps around her waist and he pulls her into him. He holds her tightly against his body. Her small dress slides up her bare ass cheeks.

"Liyan, I was really starting to like you," Chamere confesses in a low tone.

Liyan's hand goes from her face to the back of her neck. He eases her backwards until her back touches his office door. "I know you were, Chamere. I was starting to like you, too."

The moment is so thick with sexual tension that it's nearly unbearable. Chamere stares at Liyan's mouth, "Why won't you kiss me? I know you want to."

"I want to do a lot of things, but that doesn't make them the right things to do."

"So, kissing me would be wrong?"

"On so many levels."

"I don't understand." Liyan continues to hold the back of Chamere's neck while he explores the space between her thighs. Her pussy is still drenched from her orgasmic encounter with Showtime.

Liyan huffs like an enraged bull, "You know, I'm so fucking mad at you for letting Showtime lick you before I could. That number one spot was mine and you know it."

"I guess it wasn't," she states sassily.

He shakes his head, "He can never make you cum like I can."

She humps her shoulders, "He did a pretty good job if you ask me."

Liyan's annoyed state gets the best of him. He spins Chamere around and holds her face against the door. "You enjoy fucking with me, don't you?" He uses his foot to aggressively spread Chamere's legs like she's due for a cavity search. He reaches around her hips to fondle her sensitive clit.

"Liyan-"

"Shut up!" He growls, stimulating her immediately. Her legs buckle from the intense feeling of his fingers edging her pearl. "I'm about to fuck with you just like you fuck with me."

He strums at her clit as he unbuckles his pants. His hard penis emerges from his designer underwear. He lays his girthy member between her butt cheeks, "I bet you want some dick, don't you?"

"Fuck, Liyan!" Chamere yells with her palms stuck to his office door. Her body twitches with satisfaction in response to Liyan's perfect clit-rubbing skills. He slowly guides his penis down her slippery crack. Her gooey pussy lips slide up and down its veiny shaft.

"Do you want me to put it inside of you?" Liyan whispers in her ear. The feel of it moving back and forth across her opening is driving her mad.

"Of course I do," she moans out. She tries to catch its head repeatedly, but Liyan moves it out of the way before it successfully eases inside of her. She becomes frustrated, "Please, Liyan! What are you doing?"

"I'm playing with you. You like playing around a lot, I notice."

Her craving for his man meat goes through the roof. Her irritation grows, "Liyan… seriously!"

"I am being serious," he smirks. He releases her without penetrating her or taking her to her sexual peak. He's using her juices to stroke his dick by the time she turns around to face him. She gawks at him in disbelief.

"You are a fucking asshole!" she shouts while fixing her dress.

He humps his shoulders this time, "That's what happens when you deny me my pleasures; I deny yours. Don't start something that you can't finish, Chamere."

CHAPTER FIFTEEN
Dino & Erica

"What a crazy fucking night!" Beyonka blurts out as soon as she joins Chamere and Erica for breakfast. Neither of the ladies acknowledge her statement. She looks taken aback, "Damn, well I guess I'm speaking for myself then."

"You're right, Bey… it was a crazy night, but not in a good way," Chamere finally adds.

Beyonka bites her bacon, "I find that very hard to believe. Every time I spotted you, you were being devoured by that fine ass brotha with all of the tattoos. What was his name, anyway?"

Chamere's face lights up as if she forgot all about Curtis. Liyan has been taking up most of her mental space since they left Club Liquor, "That was Showtime. You don't know him?"

She shakes her head, "Nope. I've never seen him before, not even around town."

"Showtime has been at Club Liquor since the beginning, but he's hardly there now. I don't think he's been there since you started going, Bey," Erica informs her.

"Well, do you know why?" Chamere inquires.

Erica humps her shoulders, "I've heard rumors, but I'm not sure how true they are. I heard that he had a sick family member from wherever he's from that he had to take care of. Then, I heard that he was in and out of jail; and I also heard that he and Liyan kept getting into it, so he kept leaving."

Chamere looks uncertain, "I don't know why, either. He mentioned something about going out of town, but we never got into the details regarding why. I guess I could have asked him."

"Like you cared. By the way you were spread eagle on that couch, it looked like the only thing that was on your mind was getting your first Club Liquor orgasm," Beyonka teases.

"So, how was it?" Erica follows up curiously.

Chamere leans back in her chair, "I won't lie: It was weird as hell at first. Showtime was fine and all, but I didn't know him well enough to be letting him do what he was doing to me." Her eyes roll when the flashback hits her, "But then, he just kept talking to me… and eating me… and talking to me some more… and eating me some more, until I squirted all over him. I was so fucking embarrassed! I've never done anything like that before."

Erica and Beyonka smile at each other, "Well, shit girl, congratulations! You have officially been devirginized by a mister. It sounds like you had an amazing time-"

"So why did you say that things were crazy, but not in a good way, then?" Beyonka questions.

Chamere sighs, "You already know why."

Both ladies roll their eyes. "Liyan's ass? I swear, I didn't know he was this damn aggravating! What did he do this time?" Beyonka asks.

"And is that who you disappeared with for the rest of the night?" Erica adds.

Chamere fills her roommates in on Liyan's emotional words and his unstable actions. Erica and Beyonka take turns voicing their opinions about Liyan and his childish behavior. Erica is mostly shocked, "I can't believe he would play with you like that! Who takes their dick out with no intention of using it?"

"I thought it was against club rules for any of the misters to expose themselves, anyway-" Beyonka pauses to think about her words, "Oh, wait… Liyan isn't a mister, he's the owner."

"He's a prick is what he is," Chamere spits out.

"Well, what are you going to do about him?"

Chamere thinks about Beyonka's concern for a second, "I honestly don't know. What do you think I should do?"

"You can't let him get away with what he did, that's for damn sure," Erica exclaims.

Chamere makes an uneasy face, "I don't know, y'all. I've already been acting out of character since I met Liyan. I think it's time to quit while I'm ahead. I'm not going to pay $500 for a membership anyway, so I might as well give it up and move on."

Beyonka and Erica both act as if they disagree, "Fuck that! He gave you a free month and I think you should take advantage of it. Since he seems to have a problem with Showtime, then link up with him again; rub that shit all in Liyan's face."

"Uh, that doesn't sound-"

"That's a great idea, Bey, and I know exactly when she should do it," Erica cuts Chamere off to add devilishly. "Monday is testing day. That's when all of the women and misters meet at the club to see the clinician. It's usually an in-and-out type of thing, but I think we should linger around until we spot your new head doctor. If Liyan wants to put on a show, then you can, too. *It's showtime.*"

$$$

Even though it's a regular Monday afternoon, the women lined up outside the examination room are dressed like it's a Saturday night. It's apparent that each lady is looking for some sort of attention…

Every lady except for Chamere.

"I don't understand why you didn't wear the outfit we picked out for you," Beyonka whispers to Chamere.

Chamere smacks her lips, "Because, what sense did it make to wear that uncomfortable shit just to come down here and get tested? Y'all look ridiculous."

Erica folds her arms as if she's offended, "How? The misters are here so we should look our best."

Chamere glares at the men performing odd jobs around the lusty space. They repeatedly walk past the women without looking their way, "Look at them; they ain't paying us no attention… not even a little bit." Her eyes land on Dino, who is gawking in their direction. She looks surprised, "Except for Dino. Dino is all in."

"Dino has been staring over here since we arrived. What did you do to him, Erica?" Erica reacts strangely to Beyonka's question. Beyonka and Chamere step closer to her, "OK, at first, I was going to leave the subject alone, but now you're starting to scare me. Is there something going on between you and Dino?" Erica looks like a cat has her tongue. Beyonka makes a shocked face, "Holy shit, it is."

Erica gets whispering close, "Look… it's nothing really. Him and I spent a couple of nights together, that's all."

"That's all! Damn, Erica, why didn't you tell us about this? Don't tell me you were paying him-"

"No! Of course not!" Erica divulges louder than she intended. She looks around embarrassingly, "I would never pay a guy to spend time with me. Are you crazy?"

"OK… so what happened, then? How did all of this come about?"

"If you must know, I've been dealing with Dino since I first became a member. I didn't have him every ladies' night, but I had him more nights than I didn't." She sighs, "Anyway, after our session the week before Chamere started coming, he asked if we could exchange numbers. I agreed, even though I didn't think anything would come of it. He ended up asking me out the next day, so we went out that night."

"And…" Chamere pries.

Erica huffs as if she's tired of being interrogated, "And then we met up. We had a great time. We hit it off so well that he wanted to go out again."

"And you said yes?"

"Of course I did."

"So, why are you giving him the cold shoulder all of a sudden? Last ladies' night, you were treating him like you didn't want to have anything to do with him," Beyonka points out.

Erica looks troubled, "I needed to put a little space between us. Things were moving too fast-"

"You fucked him, didn't you?" Beyonka blurts out. Erica covers her face with shame. Beyonka and Chamere's jaws hit the floor, "Oh my fucking gosh, you did."

"Next!" Sharee shouts, drawing the women's attention from their juicy conversation to the examination room door. Erica realizes that it's her turn.

"I gotta go," she mumbles as she proceeds towards the clinician. They walk inside the medical office and close the door.

Beyonka stares at Chamere, "What the fuck is going on around here?"

CHAPTER SIXTEEN
Positive

"I can't fucking believe her!" Beyonka exclaims for the fourth time.

Chamere shakes her head, "What's so wrong with her fucking Dino? Hell, he has swallowed her DNA so much, they're practically married."

"No, I'm not shocked because she fucked him; Shid, I'd fuck Stallion tomorrow if he was down for it. I'm shocked because she didn't tell me! Like, damn, Erica! We talked about our fantasies involving the misters all of the time. I can't believe she finally got one and failed to tell me about it."

"Maybe there was a good reason why she didn't bring it up."

"I can't think of one possibility…"

The sight of a crying Erica emerging from the examination room halts Beyonka's words. Beyonka and Chamere rush towards her, "Oh my gosh, are you OK?"

"I need to go," Erica mutters through her sobbing. The ladies walk her towards the exit.

"Erica," Dino exclaims once he notices her tears. He jogs to her aide.

She stops him, "Not now, Dino."

"I'm just trying to make sure you're OK, that's all."

"I'll be fine," she replies.

He takes a step towards her, "Look, if there is anything I can do-"

"Believe me, you've done enough," she states nastily. He sighs before stepping to the side to let her pass.

"Well, I hope you feel better," he mutters to her from behind. The ladies proceed towards the sunlight until they are completely outside.

They get out of Big Bubba's ear range before Beyonka speaks, "Why are you crying? What happened in there?"

"I don't want to talk about it," Erica mumbles. Beyonka stops in her tracks.

"Hell no, that's not going to fly. You went in there for an STD test, and you came out crying. Tell us what the hell is going on, Erica."

Chamere looks concerned, "Yeah. If Dino gave you something, then-"

"Dino did give me something, but it's not what you think." The ladies stare at her as if they're waiting for her to explain. She wipes away her tears, "After I finished the STD test, I told the clinician that I haven't been feeling well. She asked me about my period, and I told her it was late, so she suggested that I take a pregnancy test."

"And…"

"And… I'm pregnant."

Beyonka and Chamere are stuck. They are so shocked that they don't know what to say. Erica stands there awkwardly, "Yeah. I can't believe it, either."

"You fucked Dino without a condom?" Beyonka questions.

Erica looks embarrassed, "It didn't seem like a big deal at the time. Since we both got tested regularly, we didn't think twice about it."

"Dammit, Erica! You definitely should've thought twice about it! Condoms protect you against more than sexually transmitted diseases. Pregnancy, too--- Hello!"

"You think I don't know that, Bey? I made an impulsive decision, alright!"

"Very fucking impulsive! Dammit, Erica!"

"What are you going to do?" Chamere asks in a calm voice. She tries to change the tone of the touchy conversation.

The tears roll down Erica's face again, "I don't know."

"What do you mean you don't know? You're actually considering giving birth to a bastard mistake by a man that eats pussy for a living? Are you fucking kidding me!"

"Bey, come on, that's enough. That's not called for," Chamere says sternly.

Beyonka tosses her hands in the air as if she's over the entire situation, "You know what? I can't even... do what you want to do. Have a million fucking mister babies if you want to. I'm going to get tested." Beyonka walks away from the girls to head back inside of the club. Erica allows the gentle breeze to brush her tears away.

"I really fucked up, didn't I?"

Chamere puts her arms around her caringly, "Come on; I'll drop you off at home."

$$$

After Chamere makes sure Erica makes it in the house safely, she returns to the club in Erica's car. She joins Beyonka near the examination room.

"Where is the pregnant beast?" Beyonka spits out angrily.

Chamere folds her arms, "You know what, Bey? You were completely out of line for the things you said to Erica. You are supposed to be her friend-"

"I am her friend, and as her friend, I needed to let her know that what she did was stupid as fuck."

Chamere balls her face up at her, "You're acting like you've never did anything stupid before."

"Not that damn stupid! Chamere, Erica has a whole human inside of her right now. Like, at this very moment, she is someone's mother. That's a huge fucking deal."

"Of course it is, but what's done is done. Did you think that yelling at her was going to magically make the problem go away?"

"No, but I'm fucking mad at her and that's how I deal with my anger."

"Well, you still owe her an apology. She's broken up right now and you should be more supportive."

Beyonka rolls her eyes, "Whatever."

Chamere looks around at the few women left in the club, "Has everyone been tested already?"

"For the most part. I just got finished a few minutes ago."

"Damn. Well, I guess it's my turn."

"It is," Liyan says from behind the ladies. They turn around quickly to face him. He notices their nasty glares.

"Relax. I simply came over here to let you know you're next. Sharee had to step away for a moment, so I'll be the one testing you. I hope that's not a problem."

"Are you fucking kidding? Of course that's a problem," Beyonka snarls.

Chamere grabs her arm. "It's OK. It's not a problem, Liyan," Chamere forces out. Beyonka smacks her lips.

Both of her friends are acting like idiots today.

Liyan grins, "Well, right this way." Chamere follows Liyan into the examination room. He closes the door behind her after she eases onto the table.

"Long time, no talk to," Liyan states as soon as their eyes meet.

She rolls hers, "Liyan, let's just get this over with."

"Damn. I didn't know it was like that between us." She ignores him. He prepares a cotton swab once he realizes that Chamere is not interested in chatting with him. He approaches her with it, "Say 'ahh'."

Chamere opens her mouth and allows him to take a sample from her inner cheek. He sticks it inside of a solution and drops the mixture on a test strip. He joins her while they wait for her results.

"Do you miss me?" He questions, stepping between her legs uninvitedly.

She tenses up, "Not at all."

He pulls her body closer to his, "Something is telling me that's not the truth."

Her heart rate increases with excitement, but she tries to play it off, "Well believe it. I don't miss you."

He shakes his head, "Damn, that's a shame." He kisses her neck softly, "Because I missed the fuck out of you." The goosebumps covering her skin catch Liyan's attention. He smirks, "You may not miss me, but your body sure does."

"Um, the results. I thought this was a rapid test," she blurts out quickly. He takes an amused step back.

"You're right; let's see if you've been cheating on me or not."

He stares at the results curiously. He turns to face her a short time later, "Your results are inconclusive."

"Stop fucking with me," Chamere replies.

He makes a serious face, "I'm for real. I can't read the results." She hops off the table to join him.

She compares her stick to the example and scratches her head, "Damn, you're right. So, what does that mean?"

"That means I have to take another sample."

"OK," she agrees, opening her mouth again.

He shakes his head, "No. I have to take a more detailed sample."

She looks confused, "More detailed? Like from…"

He nods his head as if he knows what she's going to say, "Yes, from there. Drop those jeans, baby. I'm going in."

CHAPTER SEVENTEEN
I Want You to...

"I think you set me up," Chamere expresses with her naked ass near the edge of the table. Liyan pulls up a rolling stool to tend to her gaped legs. "Do you know what you're doing?"

"Why wouldn't I? One thing I'm a professional at is extracting secretions from a vagina." He chuckles at his answer, but she doesn't. He licks his lips at the thought of tasting her, "I wish I could take the credit for this one, but this is all the universe's doing."

"Mmhmm," she hums skeptically. He parts her lips with his bare fingers. She jumps. "Liyan, where are your gloves?"

"I know you just saw me wash my hands. We're good."

"But what about my inconclusive results?"

"Chamere, I know you don't have anything, but legally, we have to follow protocol. Besides, I play between your legs enough to know you're not tainted."

Chamere is not sure why, but Liyan's last statement turned her on drastically. Liyan notices immediately, "Damn, I guess I won't be needing the lubricant." He takes a sample from her inner walls and places it in a new batch of solution. He returns to her drooling pussy after he adds the mixture to the strip. "I swear, I am having the hardest time fighting the urge to eat you."

Her pussy throbs from his words. "That would be inappropriate," she tries to convince herself more than him.

His hands wrap around her waist, "If you really thought that, then why are you still laying here with your pussy in my face? I already collected your sample."

"You're right; you have," she says in a shaky voice. She flinches when his soft lips press against her inner thigh.

"If you want me to eat you, Chamere, you're going to have to ask me to." Chamere swallows hard. Her clit is so swollen that it hurts. If he licks it for just a few seconds, she'll surely cum.

"I…" she starts, even though she knows she shouldn't.

He kisses her inner thigh again, "Say it."

"I want you to…"

He licks her flavor from her outer lips, "You want me to do what?"

"I want you to-"

"What the fuck is going on in here?" Chamere pops up at the sound of Sharee's voice. The clinician stands in the doorway in shock. Liyan spins around in the chair to face her.

"I'm completing an exam."

"You motherfucka! Is this why you asked me to run an errand, so you could be alone with her?" Chamere looks surprised by Sharee's accusation. She hurries to put on her underwear and pants.

Liyan finally stands to his feet, "Sharee, calm down. Let's talk about this."

"Fuck you, Liyan! I'm done talking to you! I swear, I should have stopped fucking with your ass a long time ago! You ain't nothing but a manipulator and a womanizer! I quit!" Sharee angrily gathers her belongings. She turns around to address Chamere, "You're a fool if you fall for his bullshit. He's going to break your heart."

Sharee slams the door on her way out. Liyan glances at Chamere, "Damn. That was intense, huh?"

Chamere takes a disgusted step away from him, "So, you did set me up. Ugh, you are a bigger asshole than I thought."

Liyan throws his hands up innocently, "I swear to you, I didn't rig the inconclusive results, but I did send her away when I knew your turn was coming up."

"Why would you do something like that?"

"Because I missed you. I wasn't lying about that, either."

The sincerity in Liyan's voice catches Chamere off guard. She successfully fights off the butterflies that are trying to appear in her stomach.

How can she still like a guy that treats women so badly?

She places her hands on her hips, "Your clinician just quit and I'm pretty sure she's crying by now. Do you care about anyone else's feelings at all?"

"I do, but not more than I care about my own."

"Figures," Chamere utters while she bumps past him.

He sighs, "Look; I'm sorry if you don't like my answers but I'm not going to lie to you. I want whatever we have to be as authentic as possible."

"Whatever we have? Who said we have anything?"

He sucks his teeth, "Come on, now. You can't bullshit a bullshitter. I know you feel something for me just life I feel something for you. There's no point in denying it."

She refuses to confirm his words as true, even though she knows they are. She rolls her eyes at him as she opens the door. He grabs her wrist before she leaves, "One more thing before you go." He wraps his arms around her like she's the love of his life. He kisses her on the cheek before whispering in her ear, "You passed your STD test. I'll see you at ladies' night."

$$$

"Hello, Chamere," she hears on her way towards Beyonka. She spins around when she recognizes Showtime's voice.

"Wow. Hello, Curtis," she greets him back. His handsome presence is a treat for her eyes. A large smile spreads across his face.

"Curtis, huh?"

She smiles back, "Oh yes. We're on a first name basis now. You've seen me naked so we're practically besties."

He chuckles, "Actually, I sucked the soul out of you so we're practically soulmates."

Chamere clutches her imaginary pearls, "Oh my."

He licks his lips, "I know, right. I can still remember your flavor on my tongue." He stares at her as if he could eat her again at this very second.

Chamere clears her throat, "Shit... Whew, it got hot in here." She fans herself, "So, what manual labor are you handling today?" She hurries to change the subject before she drags him to the bathroom for round two.

He glances behind him, "I have been tasked with steam cleaning that sofa." He points at the velvety couch he ate Chamere on. The sight of it gives her a flashback that causes all of her blood to rush to her clitoris.

She closes her legs tightly, "Oh, really? Did I have something to do with that?"

He stares at her seductively, "You know you did. You squirted on the absorbent furniture instead of the leather furniture. That's the rule my boss so inappropriately brought up in front of you. That guy…" Showtime shakes his head at the thought of Liyan. "Anyway, it's a nightmare trying to get cum out of suede."

She ignores his mention of Liyan and the lust growing within her. "Damn, my bad, Curtis. I didn't mean to make you work so hard."

He steps closer to her, "Don't be sorry, gorgeous. I'll clean a hundred sofas if you cum in my mouth again just like you did before."

Fuck.

"Chamere, are you ready?" Beyonka asks as she approaches Chamere and Showtime. Beyonka is clearly impressed by Showtime's sex appeal. She takes in his manly build.

"Yup. I was just chatting with Showtime. Showtime, this is my friend, Beyonka."

"It's nice to meet you," his masculine voice rings out.

Beyonka can't help but to blush, "It's nice to meet you, too."

"Alright, bestie… I guess I'll catch you later," Chamere jokes.

Curtis grins, "Until next time, soulmate."

Beyonka loops her arm through Chamere's while they move towards the exit. She leans in, "You must not have seen the way Liyan was looking at you while you were talking to Showtime. I had to come and get you before he snatched your ass up. It looked like he was ready to pounce."

Chamere looks over her shoulder and spots Liyan gawking in her direction. He stares at her seriously as if the conversation she just had with Showtime got under his skin. She addresses Beyonka, "Well, it was y'all idea to throw Showtime in Liyan's face."

Beyonka agrees, "It was, and it looks like it may be working."

CHAPTER EIGHTEEN
Cousins

"Erica," Chamere calls out after she knocks at her room door.

"Yes?" Erica answers in a sad voice.

"Can I come in?"

"Sure."

Erica is sitting up in her bed when Chamere enters. Chamere clicks on the light to reveal the balls of used tissue outlining Erica's body. Erica picks them up embarrassingly.

"I would ask how you're doing, but I think I know already." Chamere sits on the edge of Erica's bed.

Erica sniffs, "Yeah, I'm a mess."

Chamere looks at her caringly, "You know you don't have to deal with this on your own, right? I'm here for you, and in her own dysfunctional way, Bey is here for you, too."

She shrugs, "I know, but I can't expect y'all to help me deal with something that I'm not even dealing with myself. I'm pretty sure I'm still in denial. Like, what if the clinician was wrong?"

"That's a valid question. A second opinion is always best. Have you made a doctor's appointment yet?"

"No. I haven't done anything but climb in my bed and cry my eyes out."

"What about Dino? Have you talked to him?"

She balls her face up at the idea, "He's been texting me, but I haven't responded. It's almost like he knows about the positive pregnancy test or something."

Chamere looks at her curiously, "Why do you say that?"

"I don't know… he's been acting different. He's been overly interested in me and how I'm doing; extra attentive like he knows something is up."

"Do you think he got you pregnant on purpose?"

Erica's eyes widen, "No! I mean--- I don't think he did." She looks confused, "Why would he do something like that?"

Chamere humps her shoulders, "I don't know, but I think you should find out."

$$$

"I don't think I can do this, Chamere," Erica blurts out as soon as they pull up at Dino's place. Erica told Dino she needed to talk to him about something important so he suggested she come over so they could do so in person.

Chamere rubs her arm, "I came with you to offer moral support. You can do this; it's the right thing to do." Erica shakes her head like she disagrees. Chamere opens the passenger side door, "Come on, girl. Let's get this over with."

"Wait," Erica calls out to Chamere. Chamere stops before she's able to step out of the vehicle, "Look, I know I haven't been the best roommate or friend to you, but what you're doing for me right now is the most thoughtful thing anyone has done for me in a long time. I want to apologize to you for being so-"

"No need," Chamere interrupts. "None of that is important anymore. The only thing that matters is our relationship now, and I've grown to care about you--- for the most part." Both women smile.

"Yeah, I've grown to care about you, too."

Chamere climbs out of the car with Erica right behind her. They glance at the two cars parked in the driveway on their way to the front door. Chamere knocks after realizing that Erica is too afraid to do so.

"One second," they hear from inside the house.

"I can't do this. I'm going to barf," Erica exclaims with a sickly look on her face.

Chamere turns to face her, "Just breathe. Try to relax… you've got this."

The door swinging open grabs both of the women's attention. Dino looks surprised to see that Erica brought company. He holds the door open, "Hello, ladies. Come in."

"Hi, Dino," Chamere says on the way past him. She freezes when she spots Showtime sitting on the living room couch with a game controller in his hand. Dino closes the door after Erica makes it inside.

"Ladies, I want y'all to meet my cousin, Curtis. Curtis, this is Erica and…" Dino pauses once he realizes that he doesn't know Chamere's name.

Curtis smiles when he sees her face, "What's up, soulmate." She appears speechless, "Of course they know me, D. You and I work at the same establishment. It's nice to see you again, ladies." He places the controller on the table before standing to his feet. The appearance of his godly being throws Chamere off drastically.

"Soulmate? Oh, so y'all must know each other really well," Dino points out with a chuckle. Showtime glares at him as if he disagrees with Dino's sarcastic tone. Dino straightens up instantly.

"So, what brings you to our place, beautiful?"

Our place?

"Um, actually, I'm here with my friend. She wanted me to ride over here with her so she could talk to Dino." Chamere turns around to look at Erica. Erica makes an uncomfortable face.

Dino grabs her hand, "Come on. We can talk privately in my room." Erica glares at Chamere like she needs her to go with her. Chamere signals that she can do this part on her own.

Chamere faces Showtime, who is hungrily taking in her body. She blushes, "You are the last person I thought I would run into tonight."

"You disappointed?" He asks sexily.

She nibbles on her bottom lip, "No. Actually, it's very much the opposite."

He steps closer to her, "So, you must've been thinking about me like I've been thinking about you, then. Our connection to each other must have brought us together."

Their gazes lock tightly. Her pussy reacts favorably to the presence of Showtime. She breaks their eye contact before her hormones get the better of her.

"I guess it's the soulmate thing," she jokes.

He grins, "Yeah, it must be."

"Uh, I had no idea you and Dino were cousins." She changes the subject like she usually does when things are getting too heavy for her.

"Yeah, hardly no one knows. It's not something we broadcast to people."

"Oh, is there a reason for that?"

"Naw. It just never comes up. Most people have no idea we're related or that we live together."

Chamere nods her head. "I get it." She looks around. "So, what are you playing?" she asks, pointing at the game console near the TV.

He sits on the couch and signals for her to join him. She eases down close to him. "I'm playing GTA. Have you ever played?"

"Yeah, but that was a long time ago." He picks up the controller and hands it to her.

"I just finished a mission so you can start the next one. Show me what you got." After a brief refresher, Chamere starts the game. Curtis watches the screen as she maneuvers through the board like a pro, "A girl that plays GTA? I think I'm in love."

Chamere giggles, "Not only can I play GTA, but I can finish this mission with my eyes closed."

"Oh, really?" Curtis appears intrigued, "Care to put a wager on that?"

"A wager?"

"Not like actual cash, but a bet."

She thinks for a second, "Hm… what would be the terms?"

"I bet that I can distract you enough to blow the mission."

She shakes her head, "Never."

He chuckles, "Bet. If I win, then you owe me dinner. If you win, then I'll take you wherever you want to go, no questions asked."

"Sounds like it's a date no matter who wins."

He smirks, "Exactly. So, are we on or nah?"

CHAPTER NINETEEN
The Bet

Showtime turns his body towards Chamere after she gets into the game. She swallows the anticipation growing with each passing second. He slowly leans in her direction. His lips caress her earlobe, causing her to flinch from the tingly feeling. He whispers, "If you thought I blew your mind at the club, just wait until I put my mouth on you tonight. I'm not stopping until you flood this fucking living room."

Shit!

Showtime slides off the couch to his knees. He removes his shirt and tosses it to the floor. The sight of his glorious body nearly causes Chamere to drop the controller. She regains her composure before she loses the game.

"Be careful. You don't want to lose the bet before it even starts," Showtime warns her amusingly.

Chamere smacks her lips, "Whatever, Curtis. It won't happen again."

"We'll see about that."

He unfastens the button on her jeans. She pauses the game suddenly when a thought crosses her mind, "Is this appropriate? Since you work at the club, I mean. The contract I signed was pretty detailed-"

He puts his hand up to silence her, "This has nothing to do with that fucking club. This bet is personal, believe me." She nods her head as if she understands even though she's almost sure she read that outside relations with a mister are strictly prohibited. She takes a deep breath before pressing play.

Oh well… let the games begin.

Her shoes and pants are off in record time. She wants to feel weird about being undressed in such a public part of their home, but the thrill of getting caught turns her on even more.

Besides, everyone inside the house has probably seen her naked ass at Club Liquor already.

Showtime spreads her legs while gawking at her patterned pink panty, "Hearts, huh?"

Chamere smiles, "Hey, they were clean and they're comfortable. Besides, I had no clue I'd be entertaining you tonight."

"No judgments here. I honestly get tired of the over-the-top sexy shit." He massages her clit through her undergarments. He glares at her lustfully, "And who's entertaining who again?"

She moans softly when Showtime's actions make her moist. He rubs her spot until her underwear is soaked with her excitement, "It's time to take these motherfuckas off."

Her legs are pointing to the sky when Showtime slides her panties off of them. Her thighs fall open once her ankles are free. "Mm, you smell so fucking edible, baby."

Showtime wastes no time lapping up her flavorful juices. Her body jerks with every movement his tongue makes. She tries to concentrate on the game, but Showtime's exquisite cunnilingus skills are defeating her. Her body shivers every time he clamps onto her throbbing clitoris. She tries her best not to push his head away, but she does so eventually.

"Oh, so you're fighting me tonight, huh?" Showtime comes up to ask. He smiles devilishly, "Good. I like a good fight. I hope you're prepared to go all 12 rounds."

He tugs at her clit hood until her hard clitoris is exposed. He tickles it with the tip of his tongue. Her body vibrates violently. She loses her grip on the controller.

The game is over.

"Shit, Curtis! That's not fair!" Chamere exclaims loudly. He slurps all over her pearl like he doesn't care about a word she's saying. He maintains his perfect suction until she cums on his tongue. She covers her mouth to muffle her orgasmic screams.

He removes his lips when her twitching starts. He glances at the TV screen, "Looks like I won."

"Chamere! Come on, let's go," Erica yells angrily when she exits Dino's room. Erica stops in her tracks once she spots Showtime resting on his knees in front of Chamere's half-naked body. She looks away awkwardly, "I'll be in the car."

Erica hurries from the house while Chamere throws on her bottoms and shoes. Showtime helps her to her feet after she finishes, "Damn, I definitely wasn't done pleasing that body yet. What was that about, anyway?"

Dino angrily stomps down the hall a short time later. Chamere cuts her eyes at him, "Maybe you should ask your cousin." Dino glares at her while she heads to the door.

Showtime shows Chamere out, "I don't know what's going on with them, but I had an amazing time. I hope you did, too."

Chamere smiles, "Absolutely. Too bad it had to end so soon. Every time I see you, it's orgasmic."

Showtime laughs, "Literally, huh?"

Chamere faces him in the doorway with curious eyes, "I have to ask: Do you ever get tired of pleasing women without getting anything in return? Like, when do you get your pleasure?"

Showtime grabs Chamere by her waist and without warning, he kisses her. His warm tongue swirls around hers passionately. The surprised look on her face quickly fades when he pulls her close to him. She wraps her arms around his neck once her desire for him grows. They make-out until Erica hits the car horn. The sound startles them both.

"Wow, Curtis… that was…"

Chamere is speechless. Showtime is, too. "Yeah, I know right."

Erica blows the horn impatiently again, "Dammit. I gotta go."

They exchange smitten grins until she turns to head down the porch steps. He grabs her hand before she does, "Even though I get pleasure out of pleasing you, the real pleasure will come whenever you decide to fully give yourself to me. I'm a patient man, baby; I don't mind waiting, but just know: When it's time for me to get mine, I'm definitely going to get it, and you won't be able to run from me, either."

Chamere doesn't know why, but his statement nearly scares the shit out of her. Getting head from a mister is one thing, but having sex with one is a whole different story.

Why is Showtime pursuing her so tough?

What if she ends up like Erica?

What about the rules?

*What about **Liyan**?*

"I- Well…" Chamere doesn't know what to say.

Showtime softens his approach after reading her demeanor, "Like I said, I'm a patient man. I will never force you to do anything you don't wanna do. When you're ready--- if you ever are ready--- I'll be waiting; but in the meantime," he kisses her softly on the cheek, "Don't forget about our bet. You owe me dinner."

CHAPTER TWENTY
Disagreements

"What the hell took you so long?" Erica exclaims through her tears. Chamere displays an alarmed expression before clicking on her seatbelt.

"I'm sorry, but I was saying goodbye to Curtis."

"I thought you came over here for me, not to get your fucking pussy ate!" Erica spits out unpleasantly. Chamere wants to be offended, but she successfully fights the reaction after considering Erica's dilemma.

"Of course that wasn't the plan, but one thing led to another, and…" Erica folds her arms angrily as if she couldn't care less about whatever it is Chamere is about to say. Chamere changes the subject, "Anyway, what happened in there?"

"I fucking hate him!" Erica shouts at the top of her lungs. The loud volume scares Chamere. She turns to face her friend.

"Erica, tell me what happened." A speechlessness immediately falls over Erica. Chamere looks towards Dino's house furiously, "Did he do something to you? I swear to God, I'll go back in there right now and fuck his ass up!" Chamere reaches for her door handle. Erica stops her.

"Don't! This whole thing is my fault! I'm the one that's stupid! I can't believe how fucking stupid I am!" Erica begins sobbing after her words. Chamere places her hand on Erica's hand.

"Erica, it's going to be OK. Take a deep breath." Erica eventually calms down a few moments later. Chamere expels a loud sigh, "Now tell me… what the hell happened in there? What did Dino do?"

"I was so wrong about him. I actually thought he cared about me. I thought that I was special!"

Chamere becomes impatient, "Erica, if you don't tell me what that motherfucker did, I'm going to go up to his front door and ask him myself."

Erica pulls off after noticing how serious Chamere looks. She talks once Dino's house is out of view, "When we first got in his room, he was all over me. He was more concerned with sticking his tongue down my throat than listening to what I had to say." She turns the corner, "I had to push him off of me to get his fucking attention. After that, I decided to just come right out and say it. There was no use in beating around the bush, so I told him; I said, 'Dino, I'm pregnant', and do you know what that asshole asked me?"

She pauses to allow Chamere time to answer. Chamere doesn't say anything, so Erica continues, "He asked me why I was telling him because he knows it's not his."

Chamere gawks at Erica as if she can't believe her ears. Erica wipes the tears that are streaming down her face,

"I was so wrong about him. I thought he really liked me. It turns out he was just using me to get off."

"Well, what did you say after he denied paternity?"

"I started crying. I told him that he was the only person I was with, and he knew that. Then, he had the audacity to say that he doesn't know anything because he barely knows me. He claims he's 100% sure he's not the father. I can't believe I put myself in this situation."

Erica's crying worsens out of nowhere. Chamere coerces her to pull over before she crashes. They switch seats for safety reasons. Chamere begins driving towards their home, "I know you're upset, but don't let anything he says break you down. He is no longer a factor in this situation. You need to do what's best for you and say fuck him. He doesn't deserve your tears."

The car gets quiet from the heaviness of the topic. The silence lingers until Chamere pulls in their driveway. Chamere shuts off the engine before engaging with Erica again, "If you need me to go to the abortion clinic with you, just let me know. I can call off of work or we can go whenever-"

Erica cuts Chamere off to speak. "What? Who said anything about an abortion clinic?"

Chamere looks confused, "Well, I assumed that you were going to get rid of it-"

"Well, you assumed wrong." Chamere seems more confused than she was before. Erica clarifies, "Was this pregnancy a mistake? Most definitely. Will I have to raise this baby on my own? More than likely; but this baby is a part of me and I'm not going to dispose of it just because the circumstances aren't ideal."

Chamere is flabbergasted, "Erica, you do know what that means, right? You are going to be a mother. Like, fully responsible for another person for as long as you live. Not only that, but you will have to do it solo." Chamere shakes her head, "I don't know about you, but to me that sounds like a hard life that you don't necessarily have to live if you just go down to the clinic."

Erica plays with her fingers awkwardly, "I don't believe in abortions--- never have. Even though I don't want to be tied to Dino for the rest of my life, I always said that if I got pregnant, I would keep it."

Chamere has a strong urge to slap some sense into her friend, but ultimately, it's her decision to make. She swings the car door open annoyedly instead. She doesn't wait for Erica as she enters the house. Beyonka is sitting on the couch in a robe and slippers.

She rolls her eyes at Chamere, "Thanks for asking me if I wanted to tag along with y'all. I know I can be bitchy sometimes, but y'all didn't have to leave me like that." Erica finally walks in as well. Beyonka pops a chip in her mouth, "Where did you hoes go, anyway?"

Chamere answers before Erica can, "We went to tell Dino that Erica was pregnant, but he shitted on her and said the baby wasn't his." Beyonka's eyes widen from the shocking news. Chamere cuts her eyes at Erica, "But none of that matters because Erica is keeping the baby regardless. Ain't that right, girl?"

"Are you fucking insane!" Beyonka yells in Erica's direction.

Erica feels attacked, "Mind your fucking business, Bey! This has nothing to do with you."

"Bullshit! I'm not going to let you ruin your fucking life because you're hormonal right now! Think logically!"

"You know what? Fuck both of you bitches! This is my body, my life, and my decision! If you don't like it, then get the fuck out of my house!"

Chamere and Beyonka are beyond taken aback by Erica's hostile ultimatum. Erica rushes towards her room before more hurtful words are spoken. Chamere and Beyonka stare at each other in awe. Chamere flops down next to Beyonka, "Wow. That was crazy. I didn't mean to hurt her feelings."

Beyonka humps her shoulders like she doesn't care, "Whatever. If she wants to fuck up her life, then that's on her." She slides another chip between her teeth, "But you heard the woman: Since we don't like it, we should start looking for a new place to stay. In about nine months, it won't be much room for us around here anyway."

CHAPTER TWENTY-ONE
An Oral Fool

Chamere decided to pull a double at work since home is not the warmest place to be nowadays. It's so much tension in the air that it could be cut with a knife.

Unfortunately, with so much hostility between the ladies, the same knife used to cut the tension amongst Chamere, Beyonka and Erica might end up in one of their backs.

Chamere rings up her last customer for the evening and follows him to the door. She's so glad it's closing time, even though she's not looking forward to stepping through a war zone to get to her bedroom. Still, she deserves a good night's rest after the day she had. She flashes a fake smile once the older gentleman leaves the store, "Have a good night, sir."

"Finally! Time to close up," she sighs to herself. She's fumbling with the door's locks until she spots a shadowy figure approaching her. Her eyes focus on the person until his face comes into view.

It's Liyan.

Chamere smacks her lips even though butterflies are fluttering in her stomach. His masculine stride halts once he makes it to the entrance. He stares at Chamere intensely through the glass door. Their eyes are fixated on each other for what seems like forever. Chamere eventually opens the store door for him to come in.

"Hey." He greets her as soon as he steps inside, "Thanks for letting me in."

She locks the door behind him, "Hey, Liyan. What are you doing here?"

He allows the question to linger longer than it should. He eventually smiles, "I was going to lie and say I was in the neighborhood, but the truth is, I missed the shit out of you, Chamere."

Chamere wants to blush, but the guard she has up won't let her. She replies, "But how did you know I was here?"

"I didn't. I guess I just hoped you were." He steps closely to her, towering over her like a sexy authoritative figure. She slowly looks up at him with submissive eyes. His apparent dominance is subconsciously turning her on. Liyan bites his bottom lip, "Don't look at me like there's a problem unless you want me to solve it."

Chamere's breathing becomes heavy. She knows better than to tread this path with Liyan, but she literally can't help herself. The sexual tension between her and him has finally reached its peak. She nibbles on her bottom lip as well, "I can look at you however I want… what are you going to do about it?"

The moments between her last words and Liyan's hand being wrapped around her throat are a blur. Liyan forces her towards the front counter and slams her ass on top of it. He holds her tightly against his body. His mouth lays on her ear. He growls, "I'm going to take what's mine, and there is nothing you can do to stop me."

Liyan snatches her work shoes off, followed by her work pants. Chamere lays near the register with a helpless look on her face. Liyan rips her underwear from her body and stuffs them in his pocket. He spreads her legs wide, "Don't fucking cum until I tell you to cum."

Liyan wastes no time placing his head between her thighs. He gives her pussy a long, mighty lick. Chamere moans at the feeling of his warm, thick tongue. She gasps once the French kissing starts.

"Fuck!" She yells in a blissful melody. He makes out with her vagina so passionately that she can hardly breathe. He bombards her clit with smooches until her pussy oozes with stretchy goodness. He plays with her love slime using the tip of his tongue. She watches its gooeyness bridge from his lips to her opening. She wants to be disgusted, but Liyan's nastiness is making her clit harder than ever.

He notices, "I said don't cum until I tell you to. Do you understand me?"

"Yes sir."

Liyan rests on his knees when he's ready to attack her clit. He holds her waist snuggly in his strong arms while his hands spread her pussy lips to capacity. He smirks once he gets a good look at her pretty pink pearl.

Making her cum is going to be a piece of cake.

Liyan's mouth surrounds her clit on all sides. He draws air through his 'O' shaped lips, allowing the cool breeze to vibrate Chamere's already swollen clitoris. Her body reacts favorably to the gesture. He does it again, "Do you like that?"

"Shit, I love it!" She blurts out unstably. Liyan rests her clit in the center of his tongue and shakes it side to side. Her body rocks with the rhythm he's providing. He pauses when her legs start shaking, "I said don't cum."

"Dammit! How could I not?" Chamere questions hysterically.

Liyan chuckles, "Alright--- if I let you cum, you can't push my head away. You have to let me keep going until I'm ready to stop. I tend to eat pussy for hours when I'm in the mood, and I've been obsessing about tasting yours for weeks."

"OK, Liyan," Chamere agrees.

"Promise me," He demands.

She swallows hard, "I promise."

Liyan grins menacingly, "Good. If you've never had a multiple orgasm before, you better prepare yourself. It's going to be a long night for your pussy, Chamere."

$$$

The green light was all Liyan needed to act an oral fool. Chamere busted her first nut 30 seconds after her promise. Liyan's ability to take her to cloud nine so effortlessly blew her mind. Her second orgasm came almost as quickly as her first.

Uhh! Liyan!" She whines out. Her body wiggles nonstop, but his hold on her makes it impossible for her to flee. Liyan devours her vagina like the king of the jungle does his prey. His face is covered in her secretions by the time she cums a third time.

"You're holding out on me," he states unpleasantly. He sucks his index and middle fingers before sliding them in her hungry opening. Her body accepts them happily, "You can squirt for Showtime but not for me? That's not going to fly."

The mention of Showtime throws her off somewhat. She's been so engulfed in Liyan that she forgot all about her time with Curtis yesterday. She wants to feel bad, but Liyan is making her body feel too positive for any negative feelings to affect her.

Maybe she'll feel differently about it later.

Liyan fingers her with amazing skill, "I want you to squirt in my mouth. I'm drinking all of that shit."

Liyan's tongue sweeps over Chamere's clit repeatedly while his fingers explore her G-spot. Her body bounces on the counter until liquid cum erupts from between her legs. Liyan creates a leak-proof seal with his mouth around Chamere's entire vagina. He continues licking on her clit while squirt constantly streams down his throat.

"Fuck!... Shit!... Liyan, damn!" The only words Chamere can produce are profane ones. Her body is trembling so hard that her muscles are getting sore. Liyan slows down his actions and removes his fingers from her insides. He licks up the remainder of any juice that runs out of her. He watches her pulsating vagina jerk with satisfaction. He uses the bottom of his shirt to clean his face. He stands to his feet and hovers over an exhausted Chamere.

He sucks her flavor off of his fingers, "I'm not full yet, but I guess that will have to do."

CHAPTER TWENTY-TWO
Minding Someone Else's Business

"I think the security stuff is in here," Chamere says when she slowly eases the supervisor's office door open. She clicks the light switch on to illuminate the room. Liyan bumps past her to get a closer look at the interior. Her body shivers from their insignificant contact.

"There it is," he points out. He moves towards a set of monitors in the corner. She follows him. He eventually smiles after looking everything over, "We're good. This store doesn't have an active security system. All of those damn cameras out there are just for show."

Chamere expels a relieved breath, "I'm glad. The last thing I need is to get fired for getting frisky at the job. I can't afford to miss out on one red cent now that I have to move."

Liyan looks at her curiously, "Have to move? What happened with your roommates?"

Chamere sighs, "That's a long story."

Liyan wraps his arms around her, causing goosebumps to form on every inch of her skin. Liyan spots the freckles but acts like he doesn't see them, "Good. That will give us something to talk about while I drive you home."

$$$

Despite what Liyan said earlier, the car ride is a quiet one. Chamere isn't engaging with Liyan on purpose. Every time she looks his way, her body gets hot and bothered all over again. He has finally put that spell on her that Keisha was telling her about.

Now, what the hell is she going to do?

"I could have sworn we had something to talk about, beautiful," Liyan exclaims in her direction.

She tries to gather herself before facing him, "Yeah, we did. My bad."

He glances at her strangely, "Did I do something wrong?"

"No, you didn't do anything wrong."

"So, what's the problem?" He glares at her as if he genuinely wants to know.

Chamere takes a deep breath when she decides to be real with him, "Liyan… I know I asked this before, but what is it that you want from me?"

He grips the steering wheel like the question makes him uncomfortable. He clears his throat, "I want you to give me whatever part of yourself you want me to have."

She shakes her head, "No, that's not what I asked. I asked you what is it that *you* want from *me.*"

Liyan sighs, "I want you to confide in me. I want you to call me whenever you need something. I want you to feed me whenever I'm craving you. I want you to be you."

Chamere processes his answer before another question emerges, "So, what do you think I want from you, then?"

He shrugs, "I wouldn't know that. Only you can answer that one."

She thinks again, "Well, I guess I mainly want you to be honest with me. You play a lot of games with a lot of women, and I don't want to be another pawn on your chess board."

He shakes his head, "Even though I completely disagree with the way you view me, I guess I can see why you would feel that way." His eyes gaze into hers for a few seconds. Her body temperature rises, "So I promise to be honest with you, no matter what, OK?"

"OK," she agrees.

"Good. Now, can you finally tell me why you have to move? I thought you and your roommates were finally getting along."

"You're right: Things were starting to look up. Even Erica and I were starting to get close… that was until we found out she was pregnant."

"Pregnant? Oh shit!"

"Exactly," Chamere confirms.

"That's so fucking crazy to me. Erica has been coming to the club faithfully for years. I've never heard of her being with a dude outside of the fellas. When did she find time to get a boyfriend?"

Chamere looks at him as if he answered his own question. He pulls into a fast-food parking lot without warning. The sudden car jerking catches Chamere off guard. He pulls into the first parking space he sees, "Chamere, please tell me you're fucking with me."

"I'm not. Erica is indeed pregnant by a mister, and she says she's keeping it."

Liyan rubs his waves in a stressful way. He turns towards Chamere, "Which one?" She gives him the same look she gave him a few seconds earlier. Disappointment floods his face, "Dammit, Dino! I can't believe he would break his fucking contract like that! That motherfucka…"

Chamere forgot all about their contracts. She instantly feels bad for spreading Erica's business. Now, Dino is going to lose his job and Erica is going to lose her membership because Chamere can't keep her big mouth closed. Not to mention, Chamere and Showtime broke their contracts as well.

Is she going to volunteer that information, too?

"There's no need to jump the gun. According to Dino, the baby isn't his."

Liyan shakes his head in a disagreeing way, "None of that matters; that shit is still bad for business. Even if he's not the father, the word will eventually get out that the fellas are fucking customers and that's not what my business is about; but if he is the father…" Liyan shakes his head like he doesn't want to consider the possibilities.

"Well… what are you going to do?" Chamere asks worriedly.

"The only thing I can do: Hold them both accountable for breaking the rules." Chamere appears bothered by his words. Liyan notices, "What is it?"

"I didn't think things through before I told you about Erica and Dino. I don't want anyone to lose their privileges because of me. I would feel terrible."

Liyan nods his head as if he understands, "I don't want you to feel terrible, Chamere, but as the owner, I have to do what's best for the club." His words take the wind out of her sail. He sympathizes with her after taking in her defeated demeanor, "Alright, beautiful, I can't stand seeing you look like that. Damn, I can't believe you have this effect on me already." Chamere giggles smitten-like, "Maybe there's another way I can get shit done without implicating you. How did you say she found out she was pregnant again?"

"I didn't, but she found out on STD test day at the club. Sharee talked her into taking a pregnancy test after Erica complained about the way she was feeling."

Liyan rubs his chin, "Hm…that works. I can use that."

Chamere is confused, "How?"

"Well, I can tell Erica that Sharee told me about the positive pregnancy test and from there, I can try to get her to tell me about her and Dino."

Chamere co-signs his idea, "You're right; that just might work."

He nods his head, "It will." He glances at a poster of a double cheeseburger stuck in the window of the restaurant. His stomach begins to growl, "How about a bite to eat before I drop you off?"

Chamere nods her head as well, "You read my mind."

CHAPTER TWENTY-THREE
Liyan's Trap

"Oh my gosh! Thank God you're home," Beyonka blurts out after barging into Chamere's room without knocking. Chamere covers her body with the towel she just used to dry off after her shower.

Chamere smacks her lips, "Dammit, Bey! Can't you knock?"

"Fuck no I can't, especially since you left me here by myself all day. It drives me crazy when I don't have anyone to talk to."

"Erica must still be angry, huh?"

Beyonka rolls her eyes, "Yeah. The wicked witch of the westside has been hitting me with death stares all day long. I've been trying to stay out of her way."

"Well, you could have picked up an extra shift at work like I did." Beyonka flops down on Chamere's bed while Chamere shimmies up her underwear.

Beyonka smirks in her direction, "Except the drug store closed at nine but you didn't drag your ass in here until after one. Either I can't tell time, or your ass went somewhere else after you got off."

Chamere tries her best not to blush while she slides her nightgown over her head. She joins Beyonka on her bed to slather on some lotion. Beyonka folds her arms, "Mm-hmm… you must have taken Showtime on that date you owed him." Chamere's face changes at the mention of Curtis. Beyonka notices, "Oh shit--- so you weren't with Showtime?"

"No. I was with Liyan," Chamere hesitates to admit.

Beyonka stares at her with disbelieving eyes. "OK, I must be missing something here. Yesterday, I thought that Liyan was public enemy number one?"

"He was, Bey, but then he showed up to my job after closing time and manhandled me like I've never been manhandled before. I've been fighting the urge to be with him for so long, but I couldn't control myself tonight. That fucking man's skills were so…"

Chamere gets spacey as she relives her hot and steamy moment with Liyan. Beyonka appears confused, "Wait--- you fucked Liyan?"

"No," Chamere answers quickly as she ties her silk scarf over her hair.

"So, what then?"

Chamere turns to face her nosy friend, "He went down on me like no guy has ever gone down on me before. That man is a fucking head connoisseur."

Beyonka giggles before shaking her head, "You finally fell into the trap that chef chick was telling you about, I see. You are officially one of Liyan's females. I can't say that I blame you, though."

Beyonka's words embarrass Chamere. Chamere turns away from her awkwardly, "I know that's how it seems, but he treats me differently than he treats them. Him and I have something special."

Beyonka rolls her eyes, "Sure you do."

Chamere gets offended, "Damn, Bey. Can you just be happy for me?"

Beyonka's demeanor softens, "Sorry, girl. Of course I'm happy for you. Liyan is fine, rich, and apparently, he knows how to make a girl's knees buckle. I'm just a little worried about you becoming emotionally tied to him, that's all."

"Don't be. Even though Liyan and I have something going on, I'm going to keep my head about it. I won't let him do to me what he does to those other women… I promise."

$$$

Ladies' night has lost its luster now that Chamere has been intimate with Liyan. She has no desire to attend another after-party, especially since she has no idea what she's going to say to Showtime once she sees him. Even though she likes Curtis, she really wants to see where this thing with her and Liyan is headed.

However, Beyonka is relentless. She begs Chamere to go to Club Liquor with her until she says yes. They dress up and climb in Beyonka's car.

"You know what, Bey? This is my first time riding with you," Chamere points out.

Beyonka sighs, "I know. I hate driving. That's one thing I'm going to miss about Erica. That heffa loved to drive. I can't believe I have to move. I've lived with Erica for almost a year. Her and I are like family." For the first time since the ladies got into it, Beyonka seems sad about the entire ordeal. She loves Erica like a sister, and it's unfortunate that this is what their relationship has come to.

"You and me both." Chamere thinks for a second, "Hey, I have an idea: How about we move in together? We get along perfectly, plus two incomes are always better than one."

"Amen to that," Beyonka agrees. She contemplates Chamere's suggestion, "Actually, that's a great idea."

Chamere smiles, "Good. I was hoping you would say that."

The ladies pull up to the club a short time later. They head towards the alley and jump in the back of the line. Worry covers Chamere's face the closer they get to Big Bubba. Beyonka notices, "Nervous?"

"Very," she admits. "What if I run into Showtime? What will I say to him?"

"First of all, Showtime is a part-time mister. He may not even be here tonight."

"But what if he is?"

"Then ignore his ass. When you see him coming, go the other way. You don't have to talk to him if you're not ready."

Beyonka and Chamere flash their gold cards at Big Bubba before entering the club. Chamere scans the wall of men as soon as she and Beyonka are in place. She spots Showtime almost instantly. He gawks at her with a smirk on his face. He mouths the words, "You're mine", in her direction as soon as their eyes meet.

Chamere swallows hard, "Oh shit."

"Yeah, I saw that, too." Beyonka shakes her head, "And I don't mean to alarm you girl, but you're in trouble."

CHAPTER TWENTY-FOUR
Time to Pay Up

"Ladies…heyyy…" Liyan says goofily from over the speakers.

"Hey!" They shout back in unison with a giggle.

"Damn, we've missed y'all. Have y'all missed us?" The room erupts with cheers of validation. Liyan chuckles, "Good, because we can't wait to cater to you tonight. Fellas…"

The misters walk towards the women with their usual sexy strides. Showtime is swiftly moving in Chamere's direction like she's his only destination. Chamere grabs Beyonka's arm, "Shit! I have to get out of here."

"Follow me," Beyonka exclaims before dragging Chamere to the women's bathroom. They step inside and close the door as if they're being followed. "Damn, that was close."

"What the hell is Liyan doing? He usually comes out of his office before he sicks the misters on us," Chamere wonders confusedly. "Plus, did you hear how short his speech was? It sounded so rushed."

Beyonka stares at herself in the mirror, "Those are good points. I don't think he's ever started a ladies' night without making himself seen and heard first."

"So, what the hell is he doing, then?"

Beyonka humps her shoulders while fixing her hair, "I don't know, but you can always climb those stairs and find out." Chamere considers Beyonka's suggestion while Beyonka finishes primping. Beyonka faces Chamere, "I'm about to go back out there. Stallion was looking exceptionally good tonight. Call me if you need me."

Beyonka leaves Chamere in the restroom by herself. She paces the floor until a group of ladies bust through the bathroom door. They startle her with their presence. Chamere exits when the women start discussing the head they just received.

Chamere glances around the corner to look over the main floor. She spots Showtime at the bar ordering a drink. She glares in the direction of Liyan's office stairs. She hurries towards them while Showtime's back is turned.

After climbing to the top, she twists the doorknob. She smiles at the thought of surprising Liyan with her presence. Her happiness immediately dissipates when her sights zoom in on the naked clinician sitting on Liyan's desk. Her back is facing Chamere, but her moans are echoing off the office walls. Chamere watches in shock until Liyan's arms wrap around her bare waist.

"Yes, Liyan," Sharee expels lustfully. Her legs are spread wide in front of Liyan's desk chair. They shiver once Liyan gives her pussy a licking that Chamere just experienced the night before.

Chamere can no longer stomach what she's seeing.

Tears form in Chamere's eyes. She wants to yell and scream, but why would she do that? Yes, her feelings are hurt, but Liyan is being the exact person that she figured he was…

Even though she was secretly hoping that she, and everyone else, was wrong about him.

She quickly removes her gold card and lays it on the floor in front of her. She's officially over Liyan and his bullshit club. She eases his door closed, heads downstairs, and moves towards the exit.

She'll wait for Beyonka outside.

Showtime steps in front of her before she's able to leave, "Where you going, beautiful? Leaving already?"

She doesn't make eye contact with him, "Yeah. I think I'm done with this ladies' night bullshit."

"Well, if you're done, then I am, too. I only came down here to see you, but if you're out of here, then so am I." He makes Chamere grin even though she's feeling crappy. He walks with her until they reach the alley. They slowly move towards the parking lot.

"I see you're the type that likes to skip out on bets. I haven't heard from you since you left my crib."

Chamere sighs, "I know. I've been so busy with work and house drama." She chooses to volunteer only part of the truth. Showtime nods his head as if he understands.

"That house drama shit is crazy. Dino told me what's going on with him and ol' girl. Getting a ladies' night member pregnant is insane."

"So, he is claiming Erica's baby?"

Showtime leads them to his car, "I'm not saying all of that, but I saw her at the crib nearly every day for almost a month. He was fucking that girl silly. It doesn't surprise me none that she ended up pregnant. I'm willing to bet that's his child."

"You and your bets," Chamere states amusingly.

He smiles, "I know, right? I might have a gambling problem."

"Might?" she asks facetiously. He chuckles.

He unlocks his car door, "Did you drive up here?"

"I don't have a car. I rode with my friend, Beyonka." He pulls a black t-shirt from the back seat and puts it over his oily chest.

"I know you're not planning on waiting for her, are you? Ladies' night just started. Do you need me to give you a ride?" He opens the driver door while waiting for a response.

She nods her head, "That would be nice." She swings the passenger door open as well.

"There is one catch, though," he blurts out before she's able to get inside.

She pauses, "Oh? And what is that?"

"You have to honor our bet right now. I'm tired of waiting for you to take me out. You owe me, woman, and it's time for you to pay up."

$$$

"Where can we eat this late at night?" Chamere questions after realizing that it's nearly three in the morning.

"My crib. I have some stuff in the fridge that can be cooked. You do know how to cook, don't you?"

Chamere laughs, "Cooking? We never said anything about me having to cook. The terms were that I take you out."

"Well, since you took so long, I'm adding interest."

Chamere laughs again, "Fine, I'll cook."

Showtime smirks, "Good. I can't wait to see what you can do in the kitchen."

The two exchange light conversation until they pull in Showtime's driveway. She follows him to the porch and through the front door. He turns on the lights.

"We have the place to ourselves. Dino will be at the club for another five hours."

"Five hours? But ladies' night ends at six."

"Right, but Liyan holds mandatory meetings after the women leave." Chamere ignores the mention of Liyan to stop herself from getting upset about him and Sharee all over again. Showtime leads her to the kitchen. He takes a seat at the small eating table, "The floor is yours."

Chamere looks confused, "But Curtis, I don't know my way around your kitchen."

"Fridge, stove, sink, pots and pans." Showtime points sarcastically while he speaks. Chamere places her hands on her hips with a smack of her lips. He stands up to join her. "I'm sorry, but I want to enjoy watching you stumble through the kitchen, making this house smell like a real home and shit. I can't remember the last time this place had a woman's touch." He wraps his arms around her waist, palming her butt with both of his hands. "The only thing I plan on touching while you're here is your body." He leans in to kiss her. Their lips brush each other's gently.

Chamere's skin gets a chill, "Fine, but you have to stay in here with me just in case I have any questions."

He eases back in his seat, "I'm not going nowhere. I planned on watching your beautiful ass is action, anyway."

CHAPTER TWENTY-FIVE
Dessert

Showtime repeatedly turns his head to the side every time Chamere bends over to look for something in the lower cabinets. Her little skirt slides up constantly, revealing her nude-colored panty underneath. At first, she felt a little weird about the quiet gawking, but it slowly started to turn her on. Now, she's putting on a full-fledged show for Showtime. He licks his lips every time her pussy print comes into view.

"That chicken smells so fucking good," Showtime mentions, breaking the silence between them.

She turns to face him, "I'm sure it will taste even better."

He licks his lips, "Will that be the only thing I'm eating tonight?"

She kicks off her heels to make herself comfortable, "No. I'm going to see what side dishes you have in the pantry."

"And what about dessert?"

Chamere nibbles her bottom lip, "I'll let you figure out what sweets you want to eat on your own."

After locating a box of flavored rice and a can of green beans, Chamere finishes their meals. She sets the plates on the table. Showtime rubs his hands together, "Thank you, gorgeous. I can't remember the last time I had a home-cooked meal that looked this good."

"Thanks," she replies proudly.

Showtime picks up a fried chicken leg and bites into it, "Damn, baby. This shit is the bomb."

She smiles, "I know it is. Eat up."

They eat heavily while conversing lightly. As soon as they finish chowing down, Showtime shows Chamere his bedroom. She seems impressed when she takes in its neatness, "Wow, Curtis. You are damn near cleaner than I am."

He closes the door behind them, "I have a huge problem with dirt and germs; I always have. I think I have OCD or some shit."

Chamere sits on his bed without his permission, "I find that hard to believe. How can someone that's a germaphobe eat vagina for a living?"

He joins her, "The STD checks have a lot to do with it. It helps to know I'm eating disease-free pussy. Besides, I don't know if you've been around long enough to notice or not, but I don't do the ladies' night gig that often. I have to be in a financial crunch to go down there, and even then, I'm very selective about who I put my mouth on."

"Oh, really? So, what made you choose me, then?"

He licks his lips at the thought of her flavor. He slides closer to her, "I could tell you were out of your element. You didn't want to be there any more than I did. Then, when you told me that none of those fools had ever served you up, I was sold. I had to be the first one to eat you."

Chamere shutters at her pleasure being the topic of conversation. She gazes into his eyes, "You're right; you were the first person to eat me at Club Liquor. Actually, you were the first person to eat me in a long time. I sorta swore off men after my ex and I broke up."

"Swore us off? Why?"

Chamere takes a deep breath, "It's a long story that I'm not in the mood to get into right now. Let's just say that I have a history of picking the wrong guys."

Showtime wraps his arm around her caringly, "Don't be so hard on yourself, beautiful. A lot of these men out here ain't shit, my cousin included. If they fucked over a woman like you, then that's their fault, not yours."

Showtime's sweet words make Chamere smile. She lays her head on his shoulder with a yawn, "I'm not going to lie, Curtis, that food gave me the 'itis. I swear I'm ready to lay down." Chamere glances in the direction of the fluffy pillows near his headboard, "Your king-sized bed seems big enough for the both of us. Can I stay over tonight?"

"I'm honestly glad you asked me that. I was thinking the same thing, but I didn't want to sound like a perv. I'm tired as hell, and I don't want to risk falling asleep on the road while driving you home; so yes, you can stay over, baby. It would be my pleasure."

$$$

Showtime offers Chamere a shirt to sleep in. She changes in the bathroom even though he has seen her nearly naked a couple of times before. Chamere returns to his bedroom just in time to watch him strip. He removes everything but his boxers. He smiles once he can no longer ignore her stares, "I can't sleep with clothes on. I've been like that since I was little."

They climb underneath his soft comforter after the lights go out. Showtime wastes no time scooping Chamere up in his arms. He holds her body closely to his chest. She tucks her head underneath his, "Wow, Curtis. You are a great cuddler."

He smiles, "Thanks. Honestly, I'm doing this more for me than you. I can't remember the last time I cuddled with someone, so I'm taking full advantage of this opportunity."

Chamere giggles, "You didn't do much cuddling with your girlfriend?"

"I did when I had one. I haven't had a girl in so long that I forget what it feels like to be in a relationship." He squeezes Chamere tightly, "You are the closest thing I've had to a girlfriend in a long time. I'm secretly enjoying every second that you're around. I hope that doesn't freak you out."

Chamere is flattered by Showtime's confession. She always has her guard up with everyone she meets, but Showtime makes her feel so comfortable that her guard is lowering on its own. She gazes at him, "No, that doesn't freak me out at all."

He places his face closer to hers, "Well, what if I told you that I'm suddenly in the mood for dessert? Would it freak you out if that dessert was you?"

Chamere shakes her head slowly, "No… actually, I think I would really enjoy that."

CHAPTER TWENTY-SIX
Raw & Uncut

Showtime's gentleness can easily be mistaken for love. He asks permission to remove her clothes before he carefully takes them off of her. Chamere's body lays completely nude underneath one of the finest men she's ever seen. His tongue softly caresses hers while they exchange kisses.

A trail of his warm saliva leads to the side of her neck. Showtime sucks near her collarbone like an unofficial vampire. Chamere scratches at his back once the feeling takes her breath away.

"Mm…" Showtime moans as his mouth explores Chamere's body. He takes her nipples between his lips like two raisins in the sun. Her back arches while he devours her breasts. Her body shivers at the thought of Showtime's head inching underneath the cover further.

"You want me to eat you, don't you?" He questions in a deep, seductive voice. He already knows she does, but he enjoys driving her sexy body crazy with anticipation. His wet tongue comes out to lick around her belly button. Chamere impatiently forces him towards her throbbing pussy. Her legs spread wide to greet his handsome face. He smirks at her strong desire for him.

Showtime takes his time to eat Chamere right. He makes love to her with his mouth, causing her to shout out in ecstasy. He knows her body so well now that he makes her orgasm without trying. He resurfaces for air after her cum gushes from her opening.

"Can I have you?" Showtime whispers in her ear. He nibbles on her neck while waiting for a reply. Chamere's body vibrates from his blissful over-stimulation.

How could she possibly say no?

She finally finds the words she's been searching for, "Do you have a condom?"

"I do," he responds, removing his boxers with a few quick gestures. His raw penis rests on top of Chamere's drenched pussy. She gasps at the heaviness of it.

Showtime sticks his hand in his side-table drawer. Chamere hears miscellaneous items being sprawled about while he searches for a rubber. She feels his chest let out a deep sigh, "Well, I thought I did." He looks at her with disappointed eyes, "I'm sorry, baby."

"Dammit, Curtis!" Chamere spits out in a disheartened tone. She hasn't had dick in forever, so fucking him was something she was really looking forward to doing. She glares at him, "Do you think Dino has one in his room?"

Showtime smacks his lips, "Come on, now. Didn't he just knock your girl up because of his lack of preparedness?"

She looks troubled, "And I definitely don't want to end up like her, that's for sure."

"Believe me… you won't."

They both seem to be stuck in mental limbo. Neither one of them moves an inch while they secretly participate in their own internal debates. They finally make eye contact, "What do you mean, I won't?"

"I mean, I'm much more responsible than my cousin. I know how not to get a girl pregnant."

"But you can't say that. What if you don't pull out in time?"

"I've never had that problem before."

"And I'm just supposed to take your word for it?"

Showtime looks offended all of a sudden, "Look, I'm not going to make you do anything you don't wanna do. If you don't trust me, then say that." He tries to get off of her, but she wraps her arms around his neck to stop him. She leans up and kisses him passionately. He eagerly kisses her back.

They make-out until Showtime's dick is rock hard. His huge log repeatedly slides between Chamere's moist pussy lips, making her lose her mind at the thought of him easing it through her pulsating opening. Showtime separates his lips from hers, "Are you sure you're OK with this?"

"Promise me you won't get me pregnant."

"I promise to do everything in my power not to get you pregnant," he says with a smile. Even though that's not exactly what Chamere wants to hear, her horny mind decides it's good enough to proceed. Showtime slides his girthy penis inside of her a few seconds later.

"Fuck!" Chamere yells out. Showtime skillfully rolls his pelvis with every thrust he makes. He grabs her hips for stability while he slides his long member deeper inside of her. His pumps are smooth and rhythmic. Her legs shiver once she realizes that his dick is much bigger than she initially figured.

Showtime reads Chamere's face perfectly. He can tell she wants all of him, but she can't fully handle its size. He strokes her gracefully while bombarding her mouth with sweet kisses. He makes her aroused enough to open up and receive him better.

"That's it… get used to this dick," Showtime moans out. He picks up his pace, causing his headboard to beat melodically against the wall. Chamere holds on to him for dear life. He pounds at her poetically until she nears an orgasm.

"Yes, Curtis! Oh my gosh!" She screams, cumming so hard that her eyes roll. Showtime slows down until her body stops spasming. He takes her to her peak repeatedly, making sure to back off after every orgasm so she can regain her composure. He picks up speed one last time.

"Fuck, baby. You feel so fucking good," he moans out. He closes his eyes tightly when his pleasure becomes his main focus.

"Are you about to cum?" Chamere asks.

"Yeah… I'm about to fucking explode!" Showtime yells as he yanks his penis from Chamere's swollen walls. Sperm squirts from his dickhead like a violent volcanic eruption. His man milk paints Chamere's stomach white. She seems repulsed by the overwhelming amount of it.

He falls to the side a few moments later. Chamere hops up and heads for the bathroom without saying a word. Showtime hears the shower running a couple of minutes later. He decides to join her.

"Do you have a washcloth?" She asks as soon as he walks through the restroom door. He opens the closet to fetch her one. She thanks him while she steps inside the tub. He gets in behind her.

He watches her wash his DNA from her brown skin. He shamelessly admires every inch of her beautiful body. She turns around to face him after some time. He wraps his arms around her waist as soon as their eyes meet, "Thanks, baby. I really needed that. I ain't busted a nut that big in a minute."

"Same here. I didn't know how much I missed being dicked down until that amazing reminder." He kisses her lips, "But I have a question, though: What did you mean when you said that I should get used to your dick? Was that something you were just saying in the heat of the moment, or…"

Showtime grins, "Or, maybe I said that because I really want you to get used to the feel of my dick inside of you. Just maybe I want to give it to you on a regular basis."

Chamere blushes, "A regular basis? Like exclusively or something?"

"Naw. Like…" Showtime spins Chamere around to face the water. He slides his stiffening dick down her ass crack. He enters her when he finds her sticky opening. She gasps from the unexpected penetration.

He reaches around her body to strum her clit at the same time. Her knees are so weak from the blissful stimulation that she'd surely collapse if it wasn't for Showtime's strong grasp. He holds her against his chest by her throat while he slowly explores her insides. He continues with a whisper, "Like two people who really like each other pleasing each other's bodies. We don't need no exclusivity clause, but if I'm fucking you, I'm not fucking anybody else… you have my word."

CHAPTER TWENTY-SEVEN
Mister Dick

Apparently, Showtime and Chamere were both lying when they said they were tired. After they finished fucking in the shower, they got in Showtime's bed and Chamere rode his dick until the sun came up. Now, Showtime has Chamere bent over with her hands gripping the headboard. He fucks her squirting pussy from the back until they hear the front door open.

"Oh shit! Is that Dino?" Chamere asks in an alarmed voice. Showtime pauses until he hears Dino walk inside of his bedroom.

"Yeah, that's his ass. We can keep going… he won't bother us."

"But won't we be too loud?"

He grins, "Naw… not if you try your best to keep it down. You're the one that needs to shout every time you cum."

Showtime puts a strong arch in Chamere's back before he starts hitting it again. Chamere buries her head in the pillow every time she orgasms. The room fills with the rhythmic sound of their sweaty bodies smacking together. Showtime feeds her dick until he cums all over her back, "Fuck, baby! Shit!"

"Gotdammit, Curtis. That has to be the last time," Chamere expresses while sliding to her stomach. Showtime grabs a towel from the floor to clean Chamere's back. He covers them up with the comforter after he's done.

"What's wrong? I wore that ass out already?"

She rolls over to face him, "If you must know, I'm getting sore. I haven't had sex with anyone in over six months, and I haven't been fucked with a dick the size of yours in… shit… never." Showtime is flattered. Chamere lays on his chest, "Just promise me that things won't change between us now that I've given myself to you. If you act anything like Dino, I swear I'll kick your ass."

Showtime chuckles before kissing her on the forehead, "I can't promise you that nothing will change, but I mean that in the best way possible. I like you, Chamere, and I think those feelings are only going to get stronger as time goes by. I really hope you feel the same."

$$$

"You bitch! We thought something happened to you!" Beyonka yells as soon as Chamere walks through their front door. Erica and Beyonka both stand from the couch as if they've been waiting up all night for Chamere to return.

She looks confused, "My bad, y'all. My phone died."

Beyonka rushes towards her, "Your phone died? Are you fucking kidding me? Why would you leave ladies' night and not tell me? I waited around after closing, but I couldn't find you! I went up to Liyan's office and everything! He said he found your membership card, but he hadn't seen you, either. God, Chamere! Your ass ain't got no car--- I thought someone kidnapped you or something!"

"Beyonka, you have to calm down. Do you always scream this loud when you're angry?" Chamere giggles after her non-serious question. Erica can't help but giggle, too.

Beyonka smacks her lips, "You know what? Fuck y'all both. I told y'all this is how I express myself."

"Maybe you should pick a better way to get your point across when you're talking to your friends," Erica suggests, clearly referring to Beyonka's loud outbursts aimed at her days earlier.

Beyonka looks embarrassed, "I know I can be overbearing sometimes, but that just means I love y'all. I'm sorry if I hurt your feelings before, Erica. That was not my intention."

"I know it wasn't, and I totally get you being mad at me. Shit, I'm mad at me, too. I can't believe I allowed myself to get in a situation like this. My grown ass knew better." Erica glances at Chamere, "And speaking of situations, who were you with last night?"

Beyonka speaks up before Chamere can, "Well, we know you weren't with Liyan because he was just as confused about your disappearance as I was, so that only leaves one possibility-"

"Showtime," Beyonka and Erica say in unison. Chamere blushes but never verbally admits they're right. Both women shake their heads.

"Dammit, Chamere! Make up your mind, would ya? Just last night, you were talking my ear off about how different you were than any other woman in Liyan's life. I thought you were going to give him a chance. What the hell happened this time?"

Beyonka puts Chamere on the spot. Beyonka bringing up the feelings Chamere expressed to her regarding Liyan makes Chamere regret ever saying them. It's clear she jumped the gun when she assumed that she and Liyan had something special after one intimate night.

She had heard too many testimonies about him being a womanizer to believe that he would treat her any differently, anyway.

Chamere decides to sit her friends down and tell them the truth about last night. Neither Erica nor Beyonka was shocked to hear about Liyan and the clinician, but their jaws were on the floor when Chamere revealed the number of times she came on Showtime's dick.

Beyonka's mouth hangs open, "I can't fucking believe this shit. You got a mister before me, and you just moved here. I'm the only chick in this house that hasn't experienced mister dick--- that's so fucking sad."

Chamere laughs, "Stop it. You can have Stallion anytime you want. That man is obsessed with you."

"He is," Erica agrees.

Beyonka thinks about their observations, "I don't know… I guess y'all could be right."

"We are right. Just don't wound up like me--- all pregnant and shit." Erica places her hand on her abdomen with her words. She turns to address Chamere after mentioning her growing fetus, "Speaking of Showtime, did you see Dino while you were over there? Ugh… I still can't believe I'm carrying that prick's child."

"I heard him come in, but I didn't lay eyes him."

Beyonka's face lights up, "Oh yeah! I forgot that Showtime and Dino are related! That shit is crazy."

Erica piggybacks off of Beyonka's statement, "That is crazy. I hope Dino's stupidity ain't hereditary for your sake, Chamere."

Chamere gestures that it isn't, "I might not know Curtis that well, but he doesn't seem anything like Dino. He's kind, sweet, and attentive. He's rough, but gentle at the same time-"

"But did he use a condom?" Erica cuts her off to ask. Chamere looks away awkwardly like she's too ashamed to answer the question.

Beyonka and Erica look at each other with stunned eyes, "Oh my fucking gosh! Chamere… what were you thinking?"

CHAPTER TWENTY-EIGHT
Little Peanut

"How are you feeling?" Chamere asks Erica while they sit in the waiting room of the doctor's office.

Erica takes a deep breath, "Nervous as hell. Even though I'm pretty sure I'm pregnant, it won't feel 100% real until the doctor confirms it. I don't think I'm ready for that."

"Newsflash, but you don't have a choice in the matter. That baby is coming, whether you're ready or not… so you might as well get ready."

Erica takes another deep breath, "You're right. I think I'm more scared than anything else. Not to mention, I never thought my first time being a mother would be so fucking ratchet. If someone would've told me a year ago that my baby's father would be a mister that couldn't care less about me or our child, I would've cussed their delusional ass out."

Chamere puts her arm around Erica, "Life is wild. One minute, you have a very detailed plan for yourself and the next minute, you're traveling full throttle down a road you never thought you'd be on. Look at me for example: I've never been one to do clubs of any kind, especially strip clubs, but here I am being intimate with not only one club dude, but two. Not to mention the emotional ties I have to 'em both…" Chamere shakes her head, "This is not what I had in mind when I moved here."

Erica looks at Chamere curiously, "What did you have in mind, then? It seems like every time we ask you anything about Chicago or your family, you never answer. Were you looking for a fresh start? Did something bad happen there? Are you running from someone?"

Erica's concern seems sincere. So sincere, in fact, that Chamere contemplates finally answering her invasive questions. She prepares herself to talk about her hurtful past, "Well, it all started when-"

"Ms. Washington," the medical assistant calls out as soon as she appears from the back office. Erica stands to her feet.

"Wish me luck," she mutters before walking towards the heavy-set lady. They disappear behind the door a few moments later. Chamere's phone rings as soon as Erica is out of sight.

It's Showtime.

"Hey, you," she answers with a smile.

"Hey, baby. How are you today?"

"I'm good. How are you?"

"I'm better now that I'm talking to you." Chamere blushes, "I haven't heard from you since I dropped you off yesterday. I was starting to think that you hit it and quit it."

Chamere laughs, "Oh, please! I slept on and off the entire day yesterday. You tired my ass out."

Chamere can hear the grin on Showtime's face, "I'm not gonna lie, I was drained, too. I stayed in bed the rest of the day myself. My sheets smelled just like you."

Chamere looks disgusted, "Yeah… me, you, our sweat and our cum. Things got really nasty between us."

"Hell yeah, they did. I can't wait for things to get nasty between us again."

Chamere giggles, "As long as you change your sheets, we can get nasty any time you'd like."

"Shid… well, if that's the case, what are you doing right now?"

"I'm at the doctor's office with Erica. She just went in the back right before you called."

"Oh, OK. Is she good?"

Chamere sighs, "As good as can be expected, I guess. This is her first prenatal appointment."

Showtime smacks his lips, "I swear, sometimes I want to punch cuz in the face. That girl shouldn't be going through that type of shit alone."

"She's not. I'm here with her, remember?" They both smile.

"Yeah… that's true. You're a dope ass friend for that one."

"I try to be." Silences lingers for a few seconds.

"Look, I know it's never a good idea to get involved in shit like this, but I feel like I need to try and talk some sense into Dino. Him treating your girl like this is embarrassing to our family. I can't let that shit slide."

"I'm all for accountability, Curtis. Do what you feel you need to do. I really hope it helps."

"It better, or I'll have to choke his ass out until he gets his shit together."

Chamere's phone beeps once she gets another call. She glances at the screen to see who it is. Her eyes widen when she notices Liyan's name. The unexpected reminder of him pisses her off all over again. She stares at his contact until it disappears, "Hello? Baby… you still there?"

She places the phone back to her ear, "Yeah--- my bad. What were you saying?"

"I asked what you were doing after you leave the doctor's office?"

"I thought I was spending time with my soulmate."

Showtime chuckles, "My soul called for you and you answered. That's what I'm talking about."

Chamere blushes, "Yeah, yeah, yeah… just be ready to come and get me when I call you."

"Baby, you know I will be."

$$$

Chamere follows Erica to her car, and they get inside. Erica hasn't said a word since she wrapped up her appointment with the OB/GYN. She stares straight ahead in a daze once she starts driving.

Chamere awkwardly addresses her, "So… how did it go? Is everything OK?"

Erica is quiet for a moment. She finally forces herself to respond to Chamere's inquiry, "Nothing is OK, and nothing will be OK ever again."

The tears run down Erica's cheeks just like she expected them to do. She stops at a red light. Chamere rubs her arm gently, "Why do you say that? What did the doctor say?"

"He confirmed it--- like, straight out of the gate. Before the guy even spoke to me, he said, 'Oh, congratulations, young lady. You're going to be a mom'." She chuckles facetiously, "I can tell my reaction caught him off guard. I started crying right there on the spot. He had to console me and everything. I was completely fucking embarrassed."

"I'm so sorry, Erica. I should have gone back there with you."

Erica continues driving, "Why are you apologizing? None of this is your fault, and you're not obligated to be there for me, either. That fucking asshole I got pregnant by is." Erica glances in Chamere's direction, "But I do want you to know that I'm very thankful for everything you're doing for me. I don't think I'm strong enough to do this on my own yet."

"No need to thank me, Erica. That's what friends are for. Between Bey and me, we'll make sure you have the support you need to have a healthy and happy pregnancy. We've got you, girl."

Erica smiles at Chamere. Chamere does the same, "Well, what else did the doctor say? Do you have a due date yet?"

"Yeah, I do. They gave me a routine pap smear, then they gave me an ultrasound. They told me that the size of the baby matched up with the date of my last period… six weeks, five days."

Chamere's eyes light up, "You got an ultrasound? Damn, I'm so mad I missed it!"

Erica gestures towards her purse, "Do you want to see it? I have a few pictures inside of my bag."

"Girl, of course I want to see it." Chamere grabs Erica's name brand purse and unzips it. The sonogram images are sitting on top of everything else. She grabs them, "Oh my gosh! It's so little. It looks like a tiny peanut."

Erica let's out a heavy sigh, "Yeah… my tiny little peanut. It's hard to believe that we all start out so microscopic. In less than a year, that little dot is going to be a real life human. Wow… I can't believe I'm nurturing a human inside of me."

For the first time since she found out she was pregnant, Erica feels positively about her growing embryo. She grins at the thought of having a mini version of herself cuddled in her arms. Chamere notices the positive moment and grins, too. The ladies bask in the good vibes until they pull in their driveway. Chamere's entire mood changes once she notices Liyan's car in front of their home.

"Is that who I think it is?" Erica asks curiously.

"Mm-hm. What the fuck is he even doing here?"

"Well, I know he ain't here for me, so…" Chamere smacks her lips at Erica's smart comment. Erica smiles innocently, "Look, you're always giving me great advice, so I'm about to give you some: Remember what you want. Remember what you just caught Liyan doing. Remember how seeing him with Sharee made you feel. He is a natural womanizer, so you have to remain emotionally grounded when you talk to him. Don't let his charm knock you off your square. You really like Curtis, so don't fuck that up for a dude who doesn't deserve you. You'll never forgive yourself if you do… trust me."

CHAPTER TWENTY-NINE
What a Mess

"Wow… you look amazing, Chamere," Liyan points out as soon as she steps out of the car. Erica smacks her lips at Liyan's predictable statement on her way inside of the house. Chamere reluctantly walks over to him.

"Thanks," she replies dryly.

Liyan is slightly taken aback by her tone, "Is something wrong?"

"What are you doing here?" Chamere asks nastily. She has no interest in engaging with him or answering his questions. Liyan takes a step towards her.

"I was concerned about you. Your membership card was found at the club and then your roommate couldn't locate you. I thought something might've happened to you."

Chamere folds her arms defensively, "Wow, that's interesting. You claim to be oh-so concerned about me, but you never called to see if I was OK. Today is the first time your number popped up on my phone-"

"A phone that you didn't answer when I called, by the way." Liyan interrupts Chamere with a voice full of attitude. Chamere can't believe her ears.

"Are you fucking kidding? You have the nerve to use that tone with me after the bullshit you pulled the other night?" Liyan looks confused. Chamere continues, "Tell me this, Liyan: Where did you find my membership card?"

"Someone found it and gave it to me."

"Someone found it and gave it to you, huh?" She giggles sarcastically, "Was that 'someone' Sharee?" Liyan appears busted when Chamere brings up the clinician. He rubs the top of his fade, "Just like I fucking thought. I saw you with her. I saw you giving her head on your fucking desk. I saw you licking on her just like you licked on me!"

Chamere stops talking once she notices that her emotions are spiraling out of control. She brushes away a tear that wants to fall. She tries to storm away from him. He physically stops her, "Chamere--- please--- let's talk about this."

She snatches away from him, "I don't want to talk to you about shit."

"But I thought we were friends?"

"We were-"

"So why are you tripping on me like we were more than that? I promised I would never lie to you, and I haven't. I told you I'm not interested in a relationship right now. I thought you understood that-"

"The truth is, I can't be friends with you. The emotional rollercoaster is too much for me to handle. I was really starting to like you, Liyan… like a lot. You were becoming more than a friend to me. My feelings were…" Chamere pauses once she realizes her emotional ties to

Liyan are too embarrassing to speak out loud. She sums up her thoughts with one statement, "I'm done doing this with you, and I'm done with Club Liquor."

She tries to walk away from him again. He rushes towards her and grabs her around the waist. He pulls her into him, wrapping his strong arms around her caringly. His comforting embrace feels heavenly to Chamere, even though she will never admit it. "Hold on, beautiful, don't say that. Please give me a few minutes to explain myself. Afterwards, if you still want to be done with me, then I'll respect that; but I can't let you make that decision without hearing me out first. If you leave me under these circumstances, it will kill me."

$$\$\$\$$$

"Where are we going?" Chamere asks in an unenthused voice. She glares at Liyan while he drives down the interstate. Somehow, he talked her into taking a ride with him to hear him out. The car turns down a dirt road before Liyan can answer.

"It's a private spot I hit whenever I need to clear my mind. It's helped me through a lot of tough moments. I'm hoping it will help me find the words I need to convince you to stay with me."

She rolls her eyes, "How can I stay with a guy I was never really with?" He sighs but doesn't respond right away. He waits until he parks near a small trail.

They climb out of his vehicle, "Chamere, I'm not good at this type of shit, so please bear with me while I try to get my feelings out." He leads her down a narrow path.

She hesitates, "You're not about to kill me, are you?"

He stares at her seriously, "I would never do anything to hurt you. I care too much about you to bring any harm your way."

Liyan's words are piercing and heartfelt. They sound so honest that they nearly knock the air from Chamere's lungs. He grabs her hand, "We're here so we can be alone. I don't want any distractions when I spill my heart out to you."

"Your heart?" Chamere repeats, trying her best to ignore the violent beating of her own. He continues to lead her towards the sound of roaring water.

"Yes, my heart. I don't know how or even when, but you are in my heart, Chamere--- and it's completely fucking terrifying."

Chamere has no idea what to say. The words she has been dying to hear come from Liyan's mouth are finally being said…

But what if he's trying to play her again?

She talks herself into remaining level-headed, "All of that sounds good and all, but if I meant so much to you, then why did I catch you tongue-fucking Sharee?"

"I know this will be hard for you to believe, but that had absolutely nothing to do with my personal life. That was strictly business for me-"

"But it was pleasure for her," Chamere cuts him off to add. Her statement lingers as they approach a small waterfall.

Liyan takes a deep breath, "I know that… and I'm starting to realize that passing out pleasure the way I do ain't a good thing."

Chamere appears confused, "What made you think it was ever a good thing?"

Liyan humps his shoulders, "I know this may sound naïve, but I always thought of it as a fair exchange. You get something out of it, I get something out of it… everyone should be happy." Chamere shakes her head at Liyan's elementary way of rationalizing things. He comments on her reaction, "That's a fucked-up way to think--- I know that now. Women always want something more… something more that I can never give them."

Chamere stares at the crystal-clear stream directly in front of her. She squats down to touch the cool water, "And why can't you give it to them?"

He squats down to join her, "Honestly, and this is going to sound so fucked up, but I never valued women enough to want anything more with them."

Liyan's words offend Chamere, even though she knew that about him already. "Damn, that is fucked up. I feel sorry for your ex-girlfriends."

"Don't, because I don't have any."

Chamere looks shocked, "You've never been in a relationship before?" He shakes his head no, "Wow… that's pretty damn sad."

Liyan sits on the ground, "You're telling me."

Chamere sits down as well, "So, what was your plan, then? To be a player for the rest of your life?"

"Not a 'player' per se. I would use the term, 'businessman', instead."

"So, you were just going to pimp misters and trick women with bomb ass head until you what? Retired?"

Liyan looks embarrassed, "That sounded so pathetic when you said it, but yeah... in a nutshell."

She shakes her head at him, "What about family? Marriage? Children? *Love?* What about your own pleasure? When do you have sex?"

"Not as often as I eat pussy," he admits. "And I never thought much about the family dynamic. Money has been my primary concern since I left my parent's house. I guess, somewhere down the line, it became my only concern."

They stop talking for a while, allowing nature's orchestra to fill the silent space between them. Chamere dares herself to ask her next question, "Why did you bring me out here, Liyan? What does all of this have to do with me?"

He hesitates to grab her hand. His voice trembles, "Everything." He takes a deep breath, "Chamere... I don't know what you are doing to me, but you've been all that I can think about. Even on that night you saw me with Sharee, I constantly had this feeling that I was doing something wrong--- like I was cheating on you or something. I've never felt that way before... ever. You've got my head so fucked up."

Liyan gawks at Chamere like she's the most beautiful woman he's ever seen. He strokes her cheek gently with the palm of his hand. They get lost in each other's eyes. Liyan slowly moves in for a kiss. Their lips…

The text alert from Chamere's phone startles them both. She digs her cell out of her pocket and jumps to her feet once she sees Curtis's text.

"Baby, you ready yet?"

She takes a step away from Liyan, "I need to go."

"Is everything OK?" Liyan asks after standing to his feet as well. He tries to reach for her, but she dodges his advances.

"Yeah, everything is fine."

"What's up with the sense of urgency all of a sudden? Who was that?"

"Look… Liyan… I can't do this with you, OK."

Liyan seems taken aback, "You can't do what with me?"

"Do this--- whatever it is you were trying to do."

His confusion grows, "And why not?"

"Because… I…" Chamere isn't sure what to say.

Should she tell Liyan about Curtis?

She decides to be partially honest, "Because, I met someone, and I really like him." The hurt look on Liyan's face is one Chamere will never forget. She immediately feels bad for him, even though his actions are what ultimately pushed her into Showtime's arms in the first place. She approaches him, "I'm sorry if-"

"Don't. I'm fine," he spits out angrily. He moves around her and heads towards his car. She eventually trails him.

My... what a mess.

CHAPTER THIRTY
Wolf Den

Showtime's dick slides snugly between Chamere's tight walls. He grinds slowly, allowing the full length of him to ease in and out of her. Chamere gasps every time she feels the tip of his penis in her stomach. Her thighs tremble on both sides of his muscular body.

"Mm-hm… let me please you, baby," Curtis moans sexily. He stares at her many faces of ecstasy with a bite of his lip. His hard masculinity is easily conquering her moist femininity. The feel of her contracting pussy signals him to pick up the pace.

"Dammit, Curtis! Uhh!" Chamere shouts. He sticks his tongue in her mouth to muffle her cries. The sweat beads covering his back make it hard for Chamere's nails to dig into his skin. His pelvis rams into hers until she sprays her excitement all over his torso.

"That's not enough," he mutters, giving her pussy a harder pounding. He's officially balls' deep inside of her. She's barely able to take it. "Cum for me, baby," he coerces between heavy breaths. Her body freezes up when she does what she's told. His perfect strokes break her orgasm dam, causing her juices to flood Showtime's bed. He holds her spasming legs open with incredible force and fucks her through her cataclysmic climax.

"Damn, Curt! Can you keep it down in there!" Dino shouts with a kick at Showtime's door. He slows his stroking when Dino's annoying interruption messes up his concentration.

Chamere slams her hands over her mouth, "Fuck! Sorry, Curtis."

He lays on top of her, "Don't apologize, baby. He's just mad because he ain't getting no ass."

"He would if he treated Erica right." Showtime shakes his head when Chamere mentions his cousin's sorriness. Chamere continues once he lays his forehead on hers, "So, you're giving up before you cum, huh?"

"There's no rush. I got all night to tear that ass up." He contemplates climbing off of her but quickly realizes that her pussy feels too good to vacate. He rolls his hips slightly instead. The feel of his mighty penis makes Chamere's body shiver.

"Dammit, Curtis… why are you so damn good at pleasing me?"

"It's a curse," he says facetiously. They both smile.

"Well, how long are you planning on teasing me with that thing?" He picks up his pace as a response, but not enough to make Chamere cum. He places one hand against his headboard to stop it from hitting the wall.

"Why are you so adamant about getting to the finish line? Are you getting tired of me fucking you already?" Showtime's dick stiffens more, making Chamere fight all urges to scream. Her legs react favorably to his skills. His ability to control her pleasure turns him on.

She tries her best to swallow her moans, "Of course not, but I can't promise that I'll be able to keep it down if you keep giving me good dick like this."

Showtime smirks, "Fuck Dino. I'll fuck you for five to seven business days if I want and he can't say shit about it."

$$$

It might not have been five to seven business days, but it was definitely five to seven hours. Showtime fucked Chamere so many times that Dino got frustrated and left. Even when they tried to go into the kitchen this morning and make breakfast, Showtime ended up screwing Chamere in front of the hot stove. Their bacon was a little burnt, but they weren't complaining.

That's simply the price you pay for porno-style sex.

"Anything you want to watch?" Showtime asks Chamere while he surfs through the channels on his bedroom TV. They finally decide to take a much-needed break from their exhaustive love making. Showtime changed the bed linen before they went to bed last night.

She glances in his direction, "Outside of your body lying on top of mine?" She leans over with her lips puckered. He kisses her passionately.

"I thought you were tired of that show?"

She quickly disagrees, "Oh no, handsome. As far as I'm concerned, it's always showtime." They both laugh.

"Actually, I'm glad you brought that up." He turns to face her as well, "I'm getting really tired of that ladies' night shit. I think it's time for 'Showtime' to retire for good."

Chamere makes a curious face, "Why?"

"Well, a lot of reasons honestly, but the main one is--- of course--- you."

Chamere is surprised but flattered. "What do you mean?"

"For starters, I'm really liking the way we vibe and I don't want to fuck that up. The last thing I need to be doing is servicing some random female when I got a dope ass chick I'm kicking it with." Chamere blushes, "Plus, since I'm such a germaphobe as you put it, the thought of mixing bodily fluids on a regular basis repulse me, disease-free or not. I think I'm finally too old for that shit."

Chamere doesn't want to admit it, but she's relieved to hear Showtime say that. Honestly, she'd be jealous if he gave another woman the sexual attention he gives her…

Even though Liyan isn't fully in her rearview mirror yet.

"Wow, things must be getting heavy between us," she jokes, even though Showtime apparently takes her statement seriously.

He gazes into her eyes, "You have no idea."

Showtime's tone makes Chamere's heart flutter. Even though their timing couldn't be worse, Chamere suddenly realizes that she and Showtime are falling for each other. The thought of it scares the shit out of her. She breaks their eye contact once the moment becomes too intimate for her to handle.

"Curtis…"

He places his finger over her lips to shush her, "You don't have to say anything. One thing the past has taught me is that the minute you try to define shit, all hell breaks loose. Let's just continue to enjoy each other, and whatever happens between us happens."

He kisses her softly to solidify their forming bond. Chamere kisses him back, even though she's terrified of the chemistry that's boiling over between her and Showtime. She's been trying her best to move on from Liyan, but the conversation they had yesterday made her more confused than ever. Liyan's heart is impenetrable, but somehow, she broke through its tough exterior without trying.

Imagine what she could do if she actually pursued him.

Showtime tucks her underneath his arm and pulls her close to him, "So, what do you think--- about me quitting the club, I mean?"

She humps her shoulders, "I think that's one hell of a decision to make. What will you do for work?"

"I'll always make money." His response is vague, but Chamere accepts it.

"OK… well, are you totally sure you want to do this for me? I mean… the thought of you leaving a job for an undefined relationship is risky."

"You don't think you're worth it?"

She ponders his question for a second, "It's not that. I mean, I love that you're willing to do this for us, but it has to be more to it than our budding romance. You said you had a lot of reasons… what are some of the others?"

Showtime sighs as if he was hoping she didn't ask about that. He reluctantly answers, "A lot of bullshit situations have changed the way I view Club Liquor. At first, working there was fun as hell. It was ideal for me back then. I was young and still trying to find myself. The only things I cared about were partying and women, and that club paid me to do both. I ain't gonna lie--- I was the man in that bitch when ladies' night first started. It was to the point where women only wanted to fuck with me a nobody else. The other dudes got jealous. That's when the drama really started."

"Drama?" Chamere inquires.

"Yup. Hella drama. Things got really bad really quick. Truthfully, my ego was out of control for a minute, and my temper was even worse, so I was fighting a different motherfucka almost every week. That's how Dino started working there; I needed someone I knew around to back me up just in case I got jumped."

"Wow! That shit sounds insane."

"Believe me… it was. I guess that's how it goes when you're dealing with a bunch of wolves inside of a den. Things are liable to get violent." He shakes his head, "It didn't help that Liyan's punk ass never tried to keep the peace at his own fucking establishment. It turned out that he was jealous of me, too. I eventually found out that I ate one of his bitches at the club one night. He was pissed, even though I had no idea she was one of his. Turns out she was mad at him about something, and she wanted to get even with him. She used me to make him angry. Go figure."

The déjà vu from Showtime's story makes Chamere sick to her stomach. What are the odds of her using Showtime for the exact same reason as the female he's telling her about?

Uncanny.

"Anyway, shit finally smoothed over, at least that's what I thought. Turns out, Liyan never let it go, even after I stopped showing up to ladies' night. I met a girl, and I really started to like her. Plus, I had personal shit going on that needed my attention, too, so it made sense for me to leave the club foolishness behind. Fast forward a few months later and she and I were dating. We weren't official, but we were damn near it. One evening, she told me she was hanging out with her girl for her birthday, and they were headed to Club Liquor. I didn't think much of it because Club Liquor is the only decent bar around here. Plus, I thought they were going on the main side, but I was wrong. Turns out, they were hitting ladies' night."

Showtime gets uncomfortable when he reaches this part of the story. He fights the anger he wants to feel once the mention of the past reopens an old, painful wound, "Somehow someway, Liyan found out that she and I were dating. He did everything he could to take her from me."

Chamere can't believe what she's hearing. Her throat burns when she asks, "Are you serious?"

"Very," he replies. "Whatever he did worked, too. He took her right from underneath my nose."

Chamere wants to cry. How was she able to foolishly stumble in the middle of an ongoing feud between

Liyan and Showtime? She feels like crap. "Well, what happened to the girl?"

"He still has her. She works for him now. She's the cook on Club Liquor's main side."

CHAPTER THIRTY-ONE
Coming Clean

"You gotta be fucking kidding me!" Beyonka shouts as soon as Chamere gossips about what Showtime told her earlier. Chamere had to get Showtime's drama off of her chest as soon as she made it in the house, "So, why would Showtime still be working at the club if all of that shit happened?"

Chamere humps her shoulders, "I have no fucking idea."

"And he said his ex-chick is now the cook? Then, that means that's-"

"That Keisha girl--- I'm well aware."

Beyonka's mind is blown, "Holy shit!" She shakes her head, "Well, did you tell him?"

"Tell him what?"

"That you were also fucking with Liyan?"

Chamere makes an alarmed face, "Fuck no! Are you crazy?"

"No… I'm actually very sane. How can you have a relationship with Showtime if you won't tell him the truth about you and Liyan?"

"I never said I won't tell him… I said I haven't." Chamere's statement is shaky at best.

Beyonka smacks her lips, "Whatever, girl. I'm just going to say this: If Showtime is half as awesome as you say he is, then you have to tell him about you and Liyan. He will never forgive you if he finds out from someone else, and believe me, the truth always comes out whether you want it to or not."

Chamere sighs after Beyonka's words. The thought of telling Showtime about Liyan scares the shit out of her, but she knows it's necessary. "You're right. We have a date tomorrow night after my shift. I'll tell him then. I just hope I don't lose him after this."

$$$

Chamere is in a daze. She's been so worried about her upcoming conversation with Showtime that she can barely think about anything else. She's so preoccupied mentally that her boss had to have a talk with her regarding her subpar work efforts. She pulls herself together enough to make it through her shift. Her anxiety shoots through the roof when her scheduled work time comes to an end.

"Maybe this is a bad idea," she mumbles to herself. She begins to have second thoughts while gathering her belongings. She repeatedly tries to talk herself out of coming clean to Showtime, but the closer she gets to the time clock, the worse she feels about not being honest with him. "Curtis is a good guy. He deserves to know the truth."

"I'll be outside in a second," she texts him as soon as she punches out. Her heart thumps anxiously in her chest on her way towards the door. She walks out of the drugstore and is slightly surprised when she doesn't spot Showtime's car. She decides to call him.

"Straight to voicemail?" She questions the situation out loud. She calls Showtime's phone again, but it does the same thing, "What the fuck?"

Where the hell is Curtis?

"Get in," Chamere hears suddenly. She's been so engulfed in locating Curtis that she never noticed Liyan's car parked a few spaces away from the drugstore's entrance.

"Liyan, what the hell are you doing here?"

"I'm here to pick you up."

Chamere looks alarmed, "What are you talking about? I never asked you to pick me up."

"You didn't have to. I came because I knew you didn't have a ride-"

"And how would you know that?" Chamere asks impatiently. She moves closer to his vehicle.

Liyan grinds his teeth, "Because… your boyfriend isn't in town anymore. He left this morning."

Chamere pauses in her tracks as soon as Liyan mentions Showtime. She swallows the lump growing in her throat, "My boyfriend?"

He cuts his eyes at her, "Yeah… Curt. What--- you thought I didn't know about you two? I can find out anything, especially if it has to do with my club." Chamere doesn't know what to say. Her mouth opens, but no words come out. Liyan breaks their eye contact before his anger gets the better of him, "You don't have to say shit. I'm here to give you a ride, that's it. I would've felt like crap if I left you standing up here alone this time of night. After this, though, you will never see me again. Now, get in the car so we can get this over with. Let's go, Chamere."

CHAPTER THIRTY-TWO
Hater

The silence in the car between Chamere and Liyan is the loudest thing she has heard in a long time. She didn't know it was possible to be so embarrassed, pissed, and sad all at once. She's embarrassed because, even though she had no intention of hiding Showtime from Liyan and Liyan from Showtime, that is ultimately what she ended up doing. Now, she has to deal with the funk of a hot-mess situation that existed well before she came to town.

Be that as it may, she's highly pissed at both men equally. She's angry with Liyan for playing with her emotions just like he did with every other woman in his life. She's especially mad for the way he changed his mind about his feelings for her all of a sudden like she was supposed to be waiting around for him to do so.

And Showtime…

She's pissed at him for leaving without so much as a goodbye. How can they share such intimate moments one second and he be gone the next? She thought they were cool enough to at least have a conversation before he left her stranded at her job.

Maybe she didn't know him as well as she thought.

Even though all of her emotions demand to be felt, the prior two can't hold a candle to how sad she's feeling right now. Sure, she and Showtime weren't exclusive, but he was very much her companion. If she didn't know any better, she would've believed she was falling in love with him. How could it be love if he skipped town on her so easily? Love or not, her heart is still broken from his abandonment.

She glances over at Liyan and realizes that she's sad about him, too. She can tell by the look on his face that she hurt him deeply, and that was the last thing she wanted to do. She had not planned on hurting anyone, honestly. Unfortunately, everyone did get hurt…

Especially her.

She tries to clear the air, "Liyan, can we talk?"

His jaw tightens, "No… we cannot."

She gets offended, "Why not? You owe me at least a conversation."

"And how do you figure that?" He glares at her seriously. She does the same to him.

"Because I didn't lead you on like you led me on. I was very much in the right for moving on to someone else. I'm sorry if I hurt you, but that's the truth. I wasn't going to wait around for you to realize that you wanted to be with me."

"That's bullshit, Chamere, and you know it. You knew from the very beginning that we had something special. I told you that-"

"Oh yeah, that was made crystal clear when I caught you with your tongue in Sharee's ass," she responds sarcastically.

He grinds his teeth, "You're one to talk about tongues in asses. I had a front row seat to you and Curt's little performance. I guess his oral skills were good enough to break your contract for, huh? His head must be all of that since you can't seem to keep your horny ass out of his bed."

Chamere's anger grows, "I know you may find this hard to believe, but there is more to life than sexual stimulation. Unlike you, Curtis is sweet, sensitive, and he listens to me. He's attentive, protective, and I-"

"Don't you dare say that you fucking love that asshole!" Liyan cuts her off to shout.

She appears taken aback, "I was actually going to say that I really care about him, but what if I did say I loved him? Then what?" Chamere folds her arms in a challenging way.

Liyan shakes his head, "Then I would say that you were more stupid than I thought." Chamere's mouth falls open as if she can't believe what he just said to her. He hurries to explain, "You don't know him, Chamere. I know you think you do, but there are a lot of things about him that you have no idea about."

"Like what?" she asks angrily.

Liyan hesitates before his next words, "What has he told you about his past?"

She thinks about the question for a moment, "A lot of things… like him being your frat brother."

Liyan chuckles obnoxiously, "That lying son of a bitch. It may be true that he pledged our fraternity, but he wasn't in college long enough to get initiated. Even after he dropped out, though, he hung around the frat house because Quan was cool with him. He was always a jealous wannabe; mad cuz he could never be one of us."

Chamere smacks her lips, "I don't know, Liyan. If you ask me, it sounds like you're hating."

Chamere's body jerks forward as soon as Liyan slams on the brakes. The vehicles behind him blow like crazy. Liyan is so upset that Chamere thinks he's going to put her out of his car. Instead, he makes an illegal U-turn in the middle of the road.

"What are you doing?" She finally asks after his startling actions nearly give her a heart attack.

He speeds down the street in the opposite direction, "I'm a hater, huh? OK…"

His tone frightens her. It takes her back to a domestic violence situation in Chicago that she tried so desperately to get away from. Even though she's never pegged Liyan as the violent type, she could always be mistaken.

She's finding out that she doesn't know much about any of the men she allows in her life.

"Liyan, you're scaring me. Where are we going?"

He ignores her valid feelings, "To my crib. I can prove to you that what I'm saying is true. I've never hated on anyone in my life, and I'm not going to start now."

CHAPTER THIRTY-THREE
Lies & Truths

"Come in," Liyan demands, cutting the light on in his house's foyer. Chamere is secretly mesmerized by the size of Liyan's home. She awkwardly steps inside.

Liyan stomps up his elegant staircase, leaving her alone on the first floor. She hesitates before stepping through the majestic corridor. She halts once she reaches a room.

"Geez…" she mumbles, gawking at the elegant furniture that beautifully compliments the lounge area. Her feet carry her across a marble floor to a sofa that is so soft to the touch, it should be illegal.

Liyan catches her stroking its pillows, "I swear… I want to be so fucking mad at you right now, but every time I see you in that uniform, it reminds me of how I dominated your pussy on the drugstore counter." She spins to face him but refuses to comment on his sexual recount. He approaches her with a book, "Here."

"What is this?" she asks curiously. She stares at the black leather binding with massive Greek letters covering the front of it.

"That's my frat book. Inside, you'll find ever brother that has ever pledged up until the moment I graduated." Chamere takes a deep breath before flopping down on Liyan's comfortable couch. She cracks the book open.

"Well…" she states after spending some time flipping through all of the pages, "You were quite the frat boy, weren't you? You and your two amigos were front row and center at every event."

Liyan joins her on the sofa, "Yeah. Those were the days. We had a ball back then. Times were so much simpler."

"I'm sure they were."

An uncomfortable silence suddenly joins their conversation. Chamere hands Liyan his book, "You don't have to say it: Yes, it is very clear that Curtis was not a part of your fraternity. I was wrong."

"No, he was wrong." Chamere turns away from Liyan after her embarrassment returns. He slides closer to her, "Look, I don't want you to think that I'm hating on whatever you have with him, but I'm telling you… he doesn't deserve you."

"And you do?" she asks sassily.

He sighs, "No… I don't, either."

She finally turns in his direction, "OK… so he wasn't 100% honest about the frat thing--- no big deal. Besides, he told me that on the night I met him. Most folks embellish a little bit at first. I'm sure if we revisited the topic now, he would willingly clear up any confusion I may have."

Liyan nods his head, "Well, did he tell you about all of the physical altercations he had at the club?"

"Of course he did. He said he had to fight a different mister ever week."

Liyan nods his head, "But did he tell you that he nearly killed one of the guys and Curt ended up going to prison because of it?" The look on Chamere's face let Liyan know that she indeed did not know that. He nods his head again, "Yup. Lennox used to dance at my club, but now he dances at O'Ryan's version of Club Liquor. Curt fucked him up pretty good."

"Why did he do it?" Chamere can barely ask. She's truly afraid of the answer, but she has to know.

"Because Curt is an egomaniac."

Chamere gets defensive on behalf of Showtime, "But what about you? He may be an egomaniac, but you're a megalomaniac. You took Keisha from him. He told me all about that, too."

"I took Keisha from him?" Liyan roars, "I didn't take her from him! She was looking for a way out of their controlling relationship. She said that Curt scared her whenever he got mad. He even grabbed her around the neck a few times. If you don't believe me, you can ask Keish yourself."

Liyan's description of Showtime's actions gives Chamere a massive case of PTSD. The tears that she has been fighting since she found out about Showtime leaving finally gush from her eyes. Her sobbing is so unexpected that Liyan is alarmed when it starts. He takes her in his arms to console her.

"My bad, Chamere. I didn't mean to upset you."

She cries hard and she cries long. She cries so freely that Liyan's shirt is completely soaked by the time she finishes. He disappears to grab her a few tissues. She cleans her face once she has them. "I'm sorry. I didn't mean to have a complete meltdown in front of you, but I guess your story triggered me. It's just… I had to deal with a lot of abuse in my last relationship and I still haven't gotten over it. Things got so bad with my ex that I fled Chicago without telling anyone where I was going. I needed to get away from him… from there. I can't believe that Curtis is…"

She stops talking once she realizes that admitting Showtime may be abusive will break her down all over again. Liyan removes his wet shirt once the feel of it becomes too icky for him to deal with. The sight of his chiseled chest distracts Chamere long enough to collect herself.

He stands to his feet, "How about I go and change and then cook us something to eat?"

Chamere glances at her phone, "Thanks, but I don't think I'm up to it. Besides, it's getting late, and after a day like this, all I really want to do is lay down."

Liyan sticks his hand out for Chamere to grab. She stares at it for a second before reaching for it. He tugs her to her feet. "Look, I feel really bad about the way all of this shit went down… really, I do. I can't let us depart on these terms. Please, at least let me make you feel better before you go."

"Liyan…" Chamere starts.

He steps closer to her, "How about I run you a relaxing bath in my jetted tub, and after that, I rub your body down with essential oils."

"That sounds heavenly, but I'm not interested in anything sexual right now-"

"This will not turn into anything sexual; I promise. This is strictly for your relaxation and your relaxation only. Let me make up for my transgressions. I'm telling you; you won't regret it."

CHAPTER THIRTY-FOUR
Bubbles & Back Rubs

Liyan may be a lot of things, but a liar is not one of them. Chamere is definitely not regretting her decision to let Liyan cater to her, just like he said she wouldn't.

His jetted tub feels heavenly on Chamere's skin. The fragrant bubbles surrounding her are a treat to her senses. The rose petals floating is, though pretty, a little too much for her simplicity. She told Liyan they weren't necessary, but he insisted. Now, she's lying back with her eyes closed. She's nearly asleep when Liyan knocks at the bathroom door.

"I just wanted to let you know that I'm ready for you--- no rush. Whenever you're done, come down the hallway to the right. You'll see me in my bedroom."

Liyan walks away right after his words. Chamere is somewhat surprised that he hasn't tried to walk in on her the entire time she's been bathing. She somewhat expected him to be his usual perverted self.

He must have meant it when he said that things weren't going to turn sexual between them.

Chamere cleanses her skin, carefully climbs out of the tub, and wraps herself in the big, fluffy towel Liyan gave her earlier. She eases the door open and slowly moves in the direction of soft music. She notices the flicker of candlelight illuminating from a room's doorway. She takes a nervous breath once she turns the corner into Liyan's room.

"Hey," he greets her with a smile. She stops in her tracks when the sight of Liyan's nearly naked body catches her off guard. His well-sculpted muscles will forever take Chamere's breath away. She still finds it hard to believe that a body as perfect as Liyan's could exist on this side of creation. His boxer briefs sit low on his waist, revealing a strong V-cut that meets at a penis that has an impressive print through the cotton material. He looks down at his pelvis after following her eyes.

"Yeah, my bad for not wearing any clothes, but oil is hard as hell to get out of everything. I hope you don't mind."

Even if Chamere did mind, she would never admit to it. She walks over to him, "Not at all. I understand."

He gestures towards his bed, "Lay down. Let me rub all over your beautiful skin until you fall asleep."

She takes a deep breath before moving towards his massive sleeping space. His headboard of colossal gold arches appears royal in nature. Its gaudy but elegant architecture matches Liyan's personality immaculately. She climbs in his bed without removing her towel. He eventually joins her after grabbing a bottle of oil from his master bathroom. He stares at her amusingly, "You know you're going to have to take that off, right?"

She hesitates to remove the only thing standing between her nudeness and Liyan's piercing eyes. He interjects after noticing her inner turmoil, "Pull it off and drape it over your bottom half. I'm tackling your back first, anyway. I'll move it when I'm ready to go down." Liyan smirks after his statement sounds a lot dirtier than he intended. He straddles her backside a few moments later, "The only thing I want you to do is relax. I'll take care of the rest."

Liyan's massaging skills are unbelievable. His sensual touch aligns with the passion he puts forth whenever he's pleasing a woman. The low music and soft lighting create the perfect atmosphere for such an activity. He takes his time to caress every inch of her smooth back.

Chamere's dilemma with Showtime keeps trying to penetrate her thoughts, but Liyan's oily hands repeatedly rub her issues away. She can't help but to think she's cheating on Showtime by being with Liyan…

Even though he did leave her high and dry without a conversation or explanation.

"How is the pressure?" Liyan asks in a deep, sexy voice. His stern caressing makes her feel secure and cared for. Chamere's clit hardens without her permission.

"It's perfect."

"Good," his hands move to the small of her back, "Do you mind if I remove your towel? I promise to be a perfect gentleman." Chamere hesitates before agreeing to go full birthday suit in Liyan's bed. He quickly removes it before she changes her mind. He climbs off of her, "Slide your body to the edge. I need to stand over you for this part." Chamere's nakedness eases towards him. He lubes up his hands once more, "Mm… damn, Chamere. Your body is breathtaking. It definitely deserves to be worshipped."

Liyan's hands waste no time feeling all over her plump ass. He massages it so well that Chamere starts to moan. Her moaning is turning him on, but he successfully ignores his desires for the time being. This is about her and her pleasure. His pleasure will have to wait.

His palms slide down the back of her thighs. He tends to each one with equal attention. Chamere is super relaxed by the time he finishes her calves. She nearly falls asleep while his strong hands massage her feet. "Roll over before you drift off. I want to get your front half before bed."

She flips her body over, no longer caring about her bare state. Liyan's eyes nearly pop out of his head once he takes in her perfect skin and marvelous feminine endowments. He climbs between her thighs, allowing her legs to wrap around his waist. His covered dick rests against her exposed vagina. Her eyes close as soon as he starts rubbing her again.

Her arms are tended to first, and then her hands. He rubs her neck and collar bone gently, "Do you trust me, Chamere?"

Her eyes open at the random question. She and Liyan stare deeply into each other's souls. The moment is becoming overwhelmingly emotional and neither party is quite sure why.

"I can't," Chamere whispers. Liyan pauses all movements as if her answer hurt his feelings.

"You can," he counters in a voice as low as hers. The atmosphere is thick with their vulnerability. Chamere's eyes well up with tears.

"How can I? You hurt people, Liyan… you've hurt me." He eases both of her arms above her head until her fingers touch. He slowly lowers his body on hers while holding her wrists in their current position. His bare chest lies on hers; her legs open wider to accommodate his masculine build. Their faces are inches from each other.

"I'm sorry for hurting you, Chamere. The truth is, I knew from the moment I saw you that you were meant to be mine, but that wasn't the scary thing." He swallows at the thought of admitting the next part. He glares into her eyes until he finds the courage to say it, "Not only were you meant to be mine, but for the first time in my life, I felt like I was meant to belong to someone, too--- you. Not some of me or a version of me, but all of me. You are supposed to be my one and only, Chamere."

A tear successfully rolls down the side of Chamere's face. She wants to believe Liyan so badly, but Liyan is a master of saying something one second and acting differently the next; not to mention, she's still trying to sort out her feelings for Showtime, even though he's no longer around to help her do so. She really cares about Liyan, but she really cares about Showtime, too.

This whole situation is incredibly confusing and frustrating!

"What am I supposed to say to that?" she asks seriously. Liyan sticks his tongue out and sensually licks her lips. He bites his bottom lip afterward.

"You know, I haven't kissed a woman in nearly a decade, but all I've been able to think about is the feel of your lips on mine…"And just like that and without warning, Liyan kisses Chamere...

And my... what a kiss it is.

CHAPTER THIRTY-FIVE
Most Eligible Bachelor

Chamere's eyes are the size of saucers when Liyan's tongue slides between her lips. The passion behind it quickly turns her shock into desire. He massages her mouth with his until his dick is hard as a rock. He pulls back before his excitement makes him escalate the steamy situation to a place where neither of them seems ready to go.

"I'm sorry if that was out of line, but I had to do that. I dream about you, Chamere. You are fucking up my mind."

Chamere is speechless not only by his words, but his actions as well. The most eligible bachelor in this small town is practically professing his love to her. Not just that, but Liyan's tongue game is of the highest quality no matter which of her lips he chooses to kiss. Her mind is officially blown by everything that is going on. He finally let's go of her wrists and slides his palms down her skin, "Keep your arms up. I'm going down to finish your massage. It's time for the finale."

Chamere does what's she told, acting as if her hands are tied to Liyan's headboard. His curious tongue slides down her neck and towards her full breasts. He suckles on each one with incredible desire. Her back arches when she nearly cums from his amazing slurping tricks.

He continues past Chamere's midsection and stops when he's face-to-face with her throbbing pussy. He looks up at her, "How would you like your pussy to be massaged?"

"It's my job to lay back and relax, remember? You decide."

Liyan smirks naughtily, "Alright. Remember you said that."

"I will." Chamere doubles down on her words without thinking about their consequences. At this point, she's in too intimate of a position with Liyan to start applying rules now. What's about to happen is definitely going to happen…

It was practically inevitable from the very beginning, anyway.

Liyan wastes no time sliding his thick tongue between her pussy lips. She gasps when the tip of it stops on top of her already excited clit. Liyan moves his tongue around in small circles, surrounding her love button with a fence of his slick saliva. He takes her clitoris between his lips once it's firm enough to nibble on.

"Oh my…" Chamere moans out, allowing Liyan's insane skills to give her an out-of-body experience. His head giving is like nothing she's ever experienced before.

If he keeps this up, she's liable to forget all about Showtime.

"You should of never gave me free reign. I'm going to make you cum all night long," Liyan finds time to say between licks. He locks on to her spot when he decides it's time to get her first nut out of the way.

"Uhh!" Chamere screams when Liyan effortlessly makes her climax. He ingests all of her juices, only to make her cum a few moments later.

"Dammit, Liyan!" Chamere's body spasms after her outburst. Her shivering doesn't stop Liyan from making her orgasm a third time. "Liyan, please slow down!" Chamere begs. Liyan slows the movement of his tongue when her thighs close tightly around his head. He allows the rest of her squirting juices to flow over his tastebuds.

"But I'm not finished yet," he admits while removing his boxers. Chamere watches as he tosses them to the floor. He slithers up her exhausted body like a snake. His dick finds her opening without warning. She freezes up as if she can't believe what's happening. He slides deep inside of her, "I guess I'll have to finish giving you a massage this way, then."

"Liyan! What are you-"

"Shh… let me relax you, baby," he cuts her off to state. His hips roll slowly, forcing his dickhead to hit every vaginal wall she has.

"Mm…" she moans after realizing that Liyan is giving her one hell of an internal massage. His steady pace makes her moisture coat his erect shaft.

"Is that enough pressure," he asks in a tone filled with ecstasy.

She fights every urge she has to lower her arms and wrap them around Liyan's neck, "Yes, it's perfect."

Liyan keeps up his thrusts for what seems like hours. Chamere subtly cums on his cock every time she's stimulated enough to do so. He continuously kisses her neck and lips in between orgasms. He conducts himself as if her pleasure is his only priority.

"Are you going to cum?" Chamere inquires after her 10th orgasm.

Liyan slows his stroking to speak, "Do you want me to cum?"

"Of course I do. I want you to feel good, too."

"I do feel good. In fact, I feel better than good. Being with you like this is all I've wanted since I met you."

"Being with me like what?" Chamere asks curiously.

"Like this… intimate and engulfed in each other. Laying here with you is exactly where I'm supposed to be."

"What are you saying?" Chamere is afraid to ask; and just like Chamere, Liyan is afraid to answer.

"I'm saying…" he starts with his thrusting coming to an end. His dick lays snuggly between her contracting walls, "I'm saying that I'm finally ready for a girlfriend, and I want that girlfriend to be you."

Chamere stares at Liyan like she doesn't know what to say. Liyan stares at Chamere like he's hoping she'll say what he wants her to say. She can't help but to ask, "Does this have anything to do with Curtis?"

"Absolutely not. If anything, he made me realize just how special you are to me. I always thought I wanted you, but now I realize it's more to it than that. I need you, Chamere, and I hope you need me, too. Please be mine."

"I don't know what to say."

"You don't have to say anything, at least not right now. I'll give you some time to think about it. I want you to make sure that being with me is what you want to do. I'm committed to giving our relationship a real shot. Don't say yes unless you're interested in doing the same thing."

CHAPTER THIRTY-SIX
Dino's Place

Seven days.

It's been seven long days since Liyan asked Chamere to be his girlfriend. Chamere has barely slept since Liyan's relationship proposal turned her world upside down. Of course she wants to be with Liyan, but a part of her can't help but wonder what happened to Showtime.

Showtime's phone is off. Even though Chamere vowed to never call him again after he left her stranded at work, she found that her worry far outweighed her urge to be petty. She called him last night just to make sure that nothing bad had happened to him. Unfortunately, her doing so left her with more questions than answers. She tried to talk herself into leaving the matter alone, but she quickly realized that she couldn't. She made up her mind to go to Showtime's place and talk to Dino. If anyone knows what happened to Showtime, it will be his cousin.

"Are you sure you want to do this?" Erica asks Chamere after they climb inside of her car.

Beyonka climbs in the back seat as Chamere answers, "Yes, I'm positive. The question is, are you sure you want to do this? Beyonka already said she would take me so you wouldn't have to see your baby's daddy."

Erica smacks her lips, "Fuck him. I ain't scared of him. Besides, I'm going over there for you, not him. As far as I'm concerned, he no longer exists. He and I have nothing to talk about."

"You do have something to talk about, and it's his baby you're carrying around in your damn womb," Beyonka blurts out.

Erica glares at her, "Who asked you, skank?"

Chamere giggles, "Come on, ladies; play nice. Let's complete our mission before you kill each other."

Erica starts driving towards a crib that she used to frequent not too long ago. The women ride quietly until Erica breaks their silence: "Is Showtime the reason why you haven't given Liyan an answer yet?"

"Good question," Beyonka cosigns.

Chamere sighs, "I want to say no, but I would be lying if I did. The truth is, Liyan is gorgeous, wealthy, skilled, and all of that but Curtis is…" Chamere can't find the words to describe the special connection that she and Showtime had. He was more than her lover; he was also her friend.

So, why would he leave her like he did?

"It sounds to me like you may not want to be with Liyan like he wants to be with you, and I can definitely understand why. He doesn't have the best track record with the ladies, plus he's a massive womanizer. He has to cut off all of his hoes, too?" Erica shakes her head as if she doesn't think he can, "You would really have to learn to trust him before you can put your all into him," she adds.

"Right; but Showtime is not the most honest guy, either. He did lie about being Liyan's frat brother. Plus, he has a temper that may or may not be under control; and let's not forget that he loves to disappear without notice like some hood magician." Beyonka places her hand on Chamere's shoulder, "Look, Liyan asked you not to half-step so I think you should respect his wishes. If you are still on the fence, it may be best to take some time to yourself to figure out how you truly feel."

Chamere takes in her friend's words, "I think you're both right. I have a lot to consider."

$$$

"He's not going to open the door if he sees me," Erica whispers to the ladies as they climb Dino's porch steps.

Chamere knocks, "He betta, or I'll be knocking until he does." The women instantly hear the door unlock from the other side, "See? What did I tell you?"

"Yeah?" Dino says after opening his door. His amazing shirtless body nearly makes the ladies forget why they showed up in the first place.

"Um…Curtis… is he here?" Chamere forces out.

"Naw. I ain't seen him in over a week."

"Well, do you know where he went?"

Dino humps his shoulders, "I can't keep up with his ass. He leaves town without saying shit all of the time. He'll be back when he comes back." Chamere lets out a defeated sigh. Dino's eyes lock with Erica's suddenly. He looks shocked as if he didn't notice her standing there until now, "Oh, hey."

"Ugh, don't speak to me. Thanks for nothing, jerk. Let's go, girls," Erica spits out nastily. She turns around to head down the porch stairs, but Dino hurries from the door to stop her. She snatches away from him once he grabs her, "Touch me again and I'll break your hand."

He puts his hands up like he didn't mean any harm, "Look, all I want to do is talk, that's all."

"We don't have shit to talk about," Erica states in the most disgusted voice her roommates have ever heard her use.

Chamere interjects, "Actually…" she quickly slides her hand inside of Erica's purse and pulls out her ultrasound pictures. She passes them to Dino, "I think you two have plenty to talk about."

Dino glances at them, "Is this-"

"My baby? Yes," Erica snaps while snatching the sonogram images from his hand.

Dino appears regretful, "Erica, I'm sorry, OK. I'm sorry for what I said and I'm sorry for how I acted. I shouldn't have treated you the way I did. I was just scared-"

"Fuck you, Dino! I can't believe that after everything we did together, you would fix your mouth to say my baby wasn't yours!" The tears burst from Erica's eyes like she was trying her best to hold them in. Dino takes her in his arms and hugs her tightly. She tries to free herself from his grasp at first, but eventually succumbs to his warm embrace. She cries on his chest until the loud commotion makes his nosy neighbors stick their heads out of their windows.

He leads her inside of his home, "Y'all can come in, too. Erica and I need a minute to finish our conversation."

CHAPTER THIRTY-SEVEN
Moving On

By finishing their conversation, Dino meant he needed to fuck Erica's brains out. Chamere and Beyonka sit on the couch awkwardly as they try to drown out the squeaking of Dino's bed.

"Damn, he's really giving it to her, huh?" Beyonka says in a slightly jealous tone.

Chamere nods her head, "That's definitely what it sounds like to me." She humps her shoulders, "Maybe they're just celebrating the fact that their child will grow up with two parents now. Dino is back in Erica and the baby's lives… that's a good thing, right?"

Beyonka humps her shoulders this time, "I don't know; I really hope so. I would hate for this to be an 'I miss you' fuck and he resorts back to his deadbeat ways tomorrow. He better have his shit together from here on out."

"I second that emotion. I'll fuck Dino up if he abandons Erica again after this," Chamere threatens.

"You and me both, sis," Beyonka agrees. Erica suddenly releases a moan that sounds very similar to the one she used to expel at Club Liquor. The memory jog does something to Beyonka. She twists hornily in her seat, "I seriously have to get me some. Do you really think that Stallion would be down for a fuck session if I asked him?"

"Hell yeah! As much pleasure as he's given you, he's probably waiting on the opportunity to get some in return."

Beyonka nibbles on her bottom lip at the thought of Stallion, "Mm… girl, I would definitely give him everything he thought I owed him and more." Both women giggles. Beyonka turns to face Chamere devilishly, "So…where is Showtime's room?"

Chamere seems thrown off by the question, "Why does that matter?"

"Because…" Beyonka jumps to her feet and heads for the hallway. Chamere reluctantly follows her, "Because, we may be able to find something in there that will tell us where his elusive ass went."

They creep past Dino's room with Beyonka leading them to the first closed door she sees. She turns the doorknob to reveal the bathroom on the other side. She closes the door back and points to another entrance, "Maybe it's that one, then."

Chamere stands in front of her when she approaches the correct room, "We can't go in there. That's a complete violation of his privacy."

"How, when he's not even here?" Beyonka bumps past Chamere and twists the doorknob. The door swings open slowly. The sight of the bare room nearly knocks tears from Chamere's eyes. Beyonka looks lost, "I thought you said this was his room. Ain't shit in here."

"Beyonka, this is his room," Chamere can barely confirm. She stumbles across the threshold slowly, taking in the barren area in disbelief. A tear successfully falls, "I--- I don't understand."

"Neither do I," Beyonka agrees when she steps in the room as well. She opens the closet door to find it empty just like the rest of the space. She glares at Chamere, "Wow, he really did take everything. I'm sorry, girl. I know how much he meant to you."

Chamere stares blankly at the spot where Showtime's bed used to be. She relives every intimate moment they shared in that very spot. She wipes her sorrows away, "I can't believe he packed all of his shit and left. I mean, how did he do that so quickly--- why would he do that?"

Beyonka walks over to Chamere and places her arm around her shoulders, "I think the only person that can answer that question no longer lives here. He's gone, Chamere, and this time, it looks like he's gone for good."

$$$

"There y'all go. I've been looking for y'all," Erica explains as soon as Beyonka and Erica emerge from Showtime's room. She and Dino are sitting in the same spots that Beyonka and Chamere just vacated to go exploring.

Beyonka rolls her eyes, "And where did you look? Between Dino's legs?" Dino and Erica both get embarrassed.

"I'm sorry, y'all. We got a little carried away."

"We could hear that," Beyonka adds.

"We just came from Curtis's room and all of his stuff is gone," Chamere blurts out in Dino's direction.

He appears confused, "What? His stuff is gone?" He hops up to check out her claims. He's just as shocked as she is when he pushes open Showtime's door, "Damn, it is gone."

The ladies follow him to see what he sees. "Well, where would he go, Dino?" Chamere asks desperately.

Dino gestures that he has no clue, "I would say he went to stay with his mom because she's been sick, but you never really know with Curt. He might have moved in with Quan… but again, it's hard to say."

"Thanks a lot," Chamere mutters on her way past him. Everyone follows her to the living room, "How can your family member move all of their shit out and relocate without you knowing about it?"

Dino looks offended, "I don't know if you know this or not, but Curt and I ain't that close. We lived together to split the bills, not because we were family. Curt has always been a loner and a troublemaker. If he finally decided to move on, then more power to him. It was well overdue, anyway."

CHAPTER THIRTY-EIGHT
Beyonka & Stallion

"So, you whore, I guess it's safe to say that you are Dino are good again, huh," Beyonka teases Erica after she pulls off from his house.

Erica blushes, "First of all, you can't call me a whore if I fucked the dude I'm pregnant by. Second of all… yeah, we're good."

Beyonka smirks, "So tell me… what words did he use to get you from planning his murder to letting him cum inside of you again?"

Erica balls her face up, "Ew! You are so fucking nasty!" Beyonka chuckles, "And if you must know, he did a ton of apologizing and begging. He let it slip-out that he and Showtime almost got into a fistfight because Dino was dissing me so hard; not only that, but Showtime actually called Dino's mom to tell her what was going on. He said she cussed him out and told him that if he didn't take care of her grandbaby, she'd disown his ass." She glances in Chamere's direction, "That's why when it's all said and done, I'm team Curtis all the way."

Chamere doesn't bother to respond to Erica's statement. Her eyes remain glued to the passenger side window. Chamere is so brokenhearted that she can't find the words to describe how she's feeling. Beyonka taps her shoulder, "I know you're hurting right now, and I know what you just found out about Showtime sucks, but at least you finally got your answer, right?"

Chamere gives Beyonka a curious look, "What answer?"

"The answer to the question that has been plaguing you since Liyan asked it. Showtime moved away, so he can no longer be considered an option. The situation is no longer heavy if you have nothing left to weigh."

Erica chimes in, "Yeah, and I know I just said that I was team Curtis, and I will secretly always be, but you and him can't even do the long-distance thing because his phone number has been disconnected. I mean, I can understand if you want to turn Liyan down to take some time to get over everything, but the only logical answer to your question now is to take Liyan up on his offer."

$$$

"You're still not ready yet?" Chamere peers in Beyonka's room to ask.

Beyonka is so anxious that she nearly jumps out of her skin at the sound of Chamere's voice. She checks her outfit for the 20th time in the mirror, "Girl, don't scare me like that! I thought you were about to tell me that Stallion was here."

"Stallion is here," Erica states from behind Chamere. Both ladies turn around while Beyonka addresses her, "Don't fucking lie to me; is he here for real?"

Erica nods her head to confirm her claims, "I'm not lying. He is outside right now parking that huge ass pickup truck he drives."

"Fuck! Go stall him, y'all. I'll be out in a minute." Beyonka forces her friends out of her room before slamming the door.

Erica giggles, "Well, it's good to see she's not nervous."

Chamere grins at her facetiousness, "I know, right. Look at y'all: Breaking y'all Club Liquor contracts to get y'all some mister dick. Liyan is going to have a fit."

The ladies proceed to the front door. "Actually, Dino said that he talked to Liyan about it and Liyan said he was cool with it. He said as long as we don't advertise it to the rest of the customers, we can do whatever we want." Chamere makes a shocked face.

Since when has Liyan been OK with people breaking the club's rules?

The knock at the door makes Erica open it. Stallion stands on the porch looking like a hunk from a cowboy-themed magazine. He holds a bouquet of roses in his hand, "Howdy, ladies. You both are looking mighty fine this evening." He produces two single roses to hand to Beyonka and Erica. They thank him before inviting him inside.

"So, Stallion, what are your intentions with our sweet Beyonka?" Chamere jokes.

He flashes his gorgeous smile, "Well, I plan on showing her a good time mainly."

"But you always show her a good time," Erica points out devilishly.

He chuckles, "No, not that kind of good time." He thinks for a second, "Well--- maybe, but not right out the gate." They laugh. "I was thinking I could take her out for a candlelight dinner, perhaps do a little dancing afterward. Maybe take a walk around my ranch if it's not too cold out."

Chamere nods her head, "It sounds like you've put a lot of thought into this."

"I did. I really like Beyonka and it's been a long time since I've been on a proper date. I just want to make sure that everything is dang near perfect, ya know?"

Both women shake their heads, "Oh yeah, we definitely get it."

"Hey, Stallion," Beyonka says softly. The women step to the side to get a better look at her. Everyone is in awe.

"Wow… you look amazing," Stallion uses his bass-filled voice to compliment her. Both of her roommates nod their heads as if they agree.

Beyonka blushes, "Thank you. Shall we?" She proceeds towards the fine man.

He sticks the flowers out in her direction, "For you."

"Aww! Thank you, Stallion. Let me put these in some water before we go." Beyonka sashays to the kitchen with a walk to die for. Stallion watches her ass like it's the only thing he plans on eating tonight. Chamere and Erica grin once they notice how smitten he is. Beyonka returns to the group a few moments later. She loops her arm into his, "Are you ready?"

"I've been ready for this," Stallion admits to Beyonka in front of everyone. Chamere and Erica blush like he was talking to them.

Beyonka tries her best to contain her excitement, "Ditto."

"Bye! Have a good time," Chamere and Erica take turns saying to the couple as they walk towards Stallion's truck. They close the door once they pull off. Chamere looks at Erica, "I can't wait to hear about their date when Beyonka gets back."

Erica smirks, "Girl, bye. That's if she ever comes back. You saw the way they were looking at each other. If they decided to move in together after tonight, I wouldn't be surprised."

CHAPTER THIRTY-NINE
Ultimatum

Erica was partially right about Beyonka; she may not have moved in with Stallion, but she did disappear with him for the entire weekend. When Beyonka never returned home after their first date, the ladies phoned her to make sure Stallion didn't do anything heinous to her. Once she filled them in on her plans to shack up at his ranch, they left the couple alone. They figured everyone deserved their happily ever after, even Beyonka. Hell, even Erica and Dino were discussing baby names.

Chamere, on the other hand, is still having a tough time giving in to Liyan. Yes, he can give her all of the physical love and luxurious amenities her heart can desire, but what about true friendship? What about a deep, mental connection? What about fucking her mind just as well as he fucks her body?

Liyan is persistent. Every night, after he finishes his daily tasks, he asks Chamere if she's ready to give him an answer regarding their relationship yet; and every night, she tells him to same thing: "I'm still thinking about it."

Sunday night is different, though. Sunday night, Liyan decides on a different approach. Sunday night, Liyan texts her, "I need to see you."

"I don't know, Liyan. I have to work first thing in the morning, and you know how inconsistent the buses run that early."

"You won't have to take the bus to work tomorrow," is the only statement he responds with.

"Why? Are you promising me a ride?"

"Yeah… something like that."

"Fine. I'll be ready in an hour."

Liyan shows up at her doorstep exactly one hour later. Erica opens the door for him, "Hello, Liyan. Please, come in."

"Hey, Erica. Thanks," Liyan replies as he enters their cozy home. His eyes take in their surroundings quickly, "Wow. I can't believe I've never seen the inside of this place before."

"What? The Golden Palace?" Erica jokes.

Liyan smiles, "Dino told me that you and he are expecting a little bundle of joy. Congratulations to you both."

Erica smiles proudly, "Thank you. I'm not going to lie to you, I'm scares shitless. I never thought I would be someone's mother this early in my life. I'm sure Dino is just as shocked as I am."

Liyan nods his head, "He told me that he is, but he's very excited as well. He never thought much about having kids before, but now that he's about to be a father for the first time, he can't think about anything else. The dude is obsessed."

Erica and Liyan are chatting when Chamere appears from her room with an overnight bag. "Wow, Liyan. You seem to know a lot about how Dino feels," Chamere mentions facetiously after making it obvious that she had overheard their conversation.

He approaches her dominantly, "But I have yet to find out how you feel, though." The air instantly becomes thick with Chamere and Liyan's relationship dilemma.

Erica clears her throat, "I should give you two some privacy."

"No need… we're headed out," Liyan states firmly. He reaches for Chamere's hand. She gives it to him.

"Don't wait up. Liyan is taking me to work tomorrow," Chamere informs Erica on her way out of the door. She waves bye to her friend. Erica does the same.

"OK. I probably won't be here myself. Dino and I were talking about doing something later."

$$\$\$\$$$

"So… Dino was the one that told you about Erica's pregnancy, huh?" Chamere inquires sarcastically as soon as they get in Liyan's brand-new car.

He pulls off, "Would you have preferred me say that you were the one that told me all of your friend's business?"

Chamere narrows her eyes at Liyan after his smart comment. "No, but you didn't have to say all of those things about Dino like they were true. You don't think she's going to ask him if he said the stuff you claimed he said?"

"They are true," he corrects her quickly. "Dino and I did have a conversation about Erica's pregnancy, and he did tell me he was very excited to be a father."

Chamere seems surprised, "But I thought you were mad at him and Erica for breaking their contracts? Now, you're acting like you almost condone their behavior."

Liyan shakes his head, "I never said I condoned shit. I was still mad at them for what they did, but what could I do about it? Especially after finding out that my girl broke her contract as well to be with Showtime."

Chamere looks away embarrassingly, "Well--- I wasn't your girl then."

Liyan perks up, "Are you saying that you're my girl now?"

"I'm not saying anything. I guess what I'm trying to say is…" Chamere is honestly not sure what's she's trying to say. She hurries to change the subject, "So, what are we doing tonight?"

"Hopefully celebrating the start of our new relationship."

Chamere smacks her lips, "Seriously, Liyan?"

He glances at her, "I am being serious. I do want to be with you, but I'm not going to beg you. If you aren't planning on saying yes to me tonight, then that's it; I'm done trying. I really care about you, Chamere, but I'm not going to keep letting you string me along. I hold myself to a higher standard than that."

CHAPTER FORTY
Titles

Chamere doesn't have much to say to Liyan after his remarks. She does possess a slight fear of losing him, but she hates that he's trying to rush her into making a decision that she's not ready to make. Still, she decides to enjoy Liyan while she does have his attention.

Besides, he's the only suitor she has left.

They pull into his crowded driveway, "Wow. I didn't know you had so many cars. I've only seen you drive one."

"You mean two?" He questions, referring to his sparkling new ride they're currently sitting in.

She smacks her lips, "You know what I mean."

He smirks, "Yeah, I like to collect cars. I've always had a thing for em' since I was a kid. They're usually in the garage, but it was time for them to be detailed so I pulled them all out."

"Sheesh, it has to be nearly a million dollars in front of your house," Chamere points out as they hop out of the vehicle.

Liyan nods his head, "Yeah… something like that."

She shakes her head, "This is just crazy. You have seven cars, and I don't have any. That's one for every day of the week."

"You do have a car," he counters quickly.

Chamere stops to glare at him, "No, I don't. Do you think I take the bus to save on gas or something?"

Liyan chuckles, "Naw, but your public transportation days are officially over with. Starting tomorrow, you will be whipping one of these babies to work. That's assuming that you know how to drive, of course."

Chamere is dumbfounded, "Wait, wait, wait... slow down. What are we talking about right now?"

He wraps his arms around her waist and gawks at her seriously, "I'm giving you a car, baby. Any one you want, it's yours."

Chamere takes a step away from his grasp, "No, Liyan. Absolutely not, I can't accept that."

"Why can't you?"

"Because! This is a car we're talking about, not a damn microwave or some shit. A car is not a small gift."

"Do you need a microwave?"

Chamere looks at Liyan weirdly, "Uh, no..."

"But you need a car, do you not?"

"Well... I-" she stutters on her words.

Liyan grabs her around her waist again, "So take the car. A gift is a gift, Chamere. There will be no strings attached, I promise; and even if you decide not to be my girlfriend, you can still have the car. Like I told you when we first met, I can fix nearly any problem you may have, and I plan on doing just that."

$$$

"This is crazy," Chamere mumbles for the fourth time in ten minutes. Liyan fills out the title to her vehicle of choice and slides it across the dining room table. He slides the pen in her direction a few seconds later.

"How many times are you going to say that?"

She stares at the paperwork, "As many times as it takes for me to process that this is really happening. Liyan, you are giving me a car."

"No--- I'm not 'giving' you a car, remember? You won't let me. Instead, I'm 'allowing you to work off the debt in any way I see fit'," he says, using air quotes to mock Chamere.

She rolls her eyes at him, "Whatever. I don't care what you say, giving someone a luxury vehicle for free is insane. Besides, I will never give you the power to hold something that massive over my head." She proceeds to sign her name on the dotted line.

He sits back in his chair, "I can tell. You're not interested in giving me any type of power."

She slams the pen down once she finishes, "Don't you have enough power in your life without needing to take mine?"

Liyan tightens his jaw, "Is there even a such thing as too much power?"

Chamere humps her shoulders, "I don't know; maybe we should ask Hitler, you megalomaniac."

Liyan grins, "Damn, there's that word again."

She grins back, "Well, if the shoe fits…"

Chamere and Liyan stare at each other in an intense and challenging fashion. Liyan bites his bottom lip, "You know, I could take you right on this table and you wouldn't be able to stop me."

Chamere's breathing slows at the thought of Liyan manhandling her. She snarls, "I would love to see you try."

Liyan wastes no time scooping Chamere up in his arms. He charged at her so fast that she hardly seen him coming. Her ass hits the heavy wooden table hard. He devours her face with his wet mouth.

"Take this off," he demands while tugging at her shirt. It nearly rips when it slides over her head. Liyan sucks on her neck immediately afterward. Chamere claws at his clothed back like an animal in heat.

"Yes, Liyan…" Chamere moans. He unfastens her jeans while leaving her a passion mark near her collarbone. Her bottoms hit the floor a few minutes later, followed by her underwear.

"Come here," Liyan growls, tugging his pants down just enough to expose himself. He rams his dick inside of her already wet vagina. The pleasure is so great, she falls back on the table. "Mm-hm," Liyan hums dominantly. He fucks Chamere with long and deep strokes. She arches her back when Liyan wraps his hand around her throat. He chokes her beautifully while feeding her every inch of him.

"I'm going to cum!" she announces suddenly. Her legs shiver violently while Liyan continues to bang her through her erotic explosion. He takes her legs and places them on his shoulders after she's done. He grips her waist strongly and pounds at her still squirting opening. He does so until his chest heaves violently.

"Fuck, Chamere! I'm cumming, too!" he blurts out. Liyan's penis is yanked out of Chamere just in time for him to skeet on the dining room floor. He stumbles backwards before he's able to regain his composure, "Shit! That was magnificent! I needed that, baby."

"So did I," Chamere agrees. They look at each other lustfully.

"This should be us all of the time," Liyan adds emotionally.

Chamere sighs, "It should, but it can't be."

Liyan gets frustrated, "But why not? Look at how good we are together."

"We have good body chemistry, Liyan, that's all. I'm attracted to you, and you're attracted to me. There is more to a relationship than great sex."

Liyan looks offended, "How fucking shallow do you think I am? Just because I've never been in a relationship before doesn't mean I have no idea how they go. Give me a little more credit than that."

Chamere sits up, "I didn't mean it like that-"

"Yeah, well--- you could've fooled me."

Chamere feels vulnerable enough to finally tell Liyan how she truly feels, "Liyan, I'm scared, OK. I'm scared that you're going to play me, or that this amazing guy you're being right now is all an act. I'm afraid that everything everyone says about you is true… that you're going to get me right where you want me, and then throw me to the side like you do everyone else. I'm afraid you're going to break my heart."

Liyan stares at Chamere like her words secretly hurt him. He swallows hard as if what he's about to say stings coming up. He finally responds, "I'm sorry you feel that way, but I deserve the chance to prove you wrong. The truth is, you challenge me more than I've ever been challenged in my life. You are so smart, beautiful, and you have a strong mind of your own. You're not impressed by the basic shit that most women are impressed by, your just so… different." Liyan pauses to collect his thoughts, "I don't know how, or even when, but somewhere down the line, I fell in love with you, Chamere. I've been trying to fight it, but the more I do, the clearer it becomes."

Chamere doesn't know what to say. Liyan's confession has literally snatched her ability to speak from her body. Liyan appears embarrassed, "I know, right. If I were you, I'd be speechless, too. It still doesn't change the fact that it's true."

CHAPTER FORTY-ONE
The Big Payback

Chamere lays in Liyan's bed while his arm is wrapped snuggly around her. After he fucked her brains out a second time, he fell asleep holding her. Now, she's lying in front of him with a troubled look on her face. Things between her and Liyan are moving in a direction that she never imagined they would go. It's one thing for him to give her a vehicle, but Liyan claims he is now in love with her, too. She's finding all of this hard to believe.

Where did this side of Liyan come from?

"Baby, you up?" She hears from behind her. The unexpected sound of Liyan's deep voice startles her.

"Yes… I'm up."

He glances at the clock on his nightstand, "It's late. You can't sleep?"

She sighs, "Not really." She spins around to face him, "Liyan, we need to talk."

"Shit. That tone doesn't sound good."

She smiles, "It will be painless, I promise."

He smiles back, "OK, then… what's on your mind, beautiful?"

"I was thinking about everything that we've been going through, and everything we've argued about, and all of the feelings we've shared… and I can't help but to wonder where all of this is coming from."

"All of what?" he asks curiously.

"All of this," she gestures with her hands. "Like, when we first met, you were this cold-hearted, selfish womanizer that only gave a damn about his club and his money. You vowed to not only be single forever, but to never fall in love. Now, you're sweet, generous, and you're actively pursuing a relationship with me… and to top it all off, you claim I'm your first-" Chamere stops talking as if she feels weird about saying her next words.

Liyan finishes her statement, "That you're the first woman I've ever fell in love with?" She nods her head as if that's what she wanted to say. He sighs, "Chamere, that's not a claim, that's a fact."

"How can it be, though? Like, how can you go from one end of the spectrum to the other so quickly?"

"Easy--- you," he answers immediately. Chamere insinuates that she's having a hard time believing him. He sighs again, "Let me ask you this, Chamere, and be honest: Is it hard for you to believe that I love you because you don't trust me, or is it because you don't feel the same?"

Liyan's question catches her off guard, even though she knew the topic of her feelings was going to come up sooner or later. She shrugs her shoulders, "I honestly don't know how to answer that question."

He challenges her response, "You do know how, you're just too afraid to do so."

"What do you mean?" she inquires curiously. Liyan slides closer to her like he wants her to listen carefully to what he's about to say.

"You don't know how to answer that question because you are too afraid to face how you really feel about me. You are so convinced I'm the villain and not the prince who is meant to sweep you off of your feet that you won't entertain the possibility of another narrative. You won't allow yourself to feel for me what I know your heart wants you to feel. Maybe that has something to do with my past, or your past, or Curt even, but that still doesn't change the fact that you're too big of a coward to look inside of yourself and sort out your feelings; and until you do that, you're going to be stuck right where you are. The only thing is, I don't plan on being stuck here with you."

$$$

"Holy shit, girl! Liyan bought you a car?" Beyonka blurts out as soon as Chamere makes it inside of the house after a long shift at work. Her loud outburst makes Chamere jump.

"Geez! Hello to you, too. How did you see me pull up anyway? What were you doing, watching cars drive up and down the street?"

Beyonka smacks her lips, "For your information, I'm waiting for Stallion to swing by and bring me some food. I was looking for his truck when I spotted you pull up in a new whip. Shit, that car is nice! What kind of vehicle is that?"

"What kind of vehicle is what?" Erica butts in when she emerges from the kitchen.

Beyonka points towards the front of the house, "The car that Chamere just pulled up in. It has 'lavish lifestyle' written all over it." Erica rushes to the window to check it out.

Her mouth hits the floor, "Damn, Chamere! That car costs more than we make in a year combined-"

"Before taxes," Beyonka adds.

Chamere giggles, "Y'all know y'all be doing too much, right?"

"So… how much dick did you have to suck to get that thing?" Beyonka jokes.

Chamere shakes her head at her perverted friend, "See, that's your problem now. All you think about is freaky shit. You betta be careful before you end up like Erica." Beyonka and Erica gesture that neither of them appreciates Chamere's words. Chamere giggles again, "I'm only kidding."

"Whatever, bitch… I'm happy," Erica responds sassily.

Beyonka cuts her eyes at her, "Now you are! Don't act like you weren't ready to burn Dino's house to the ground less than two weeks ago. The only thing that saved his ass was the fact that Showtime lived there." Beyonka pauses with embarrassment once she brings up a sore subject for Chamere, "Well… used to live there. Sorry, girl. I shouldn't have brought that up."

Chamere tries her best to act like the mention of Showtime doesn't faze her, "No need to apologize. It's no big deal."

"We can see that by the way you dipped with Liyan last night," Erica points out.

"And by the looks of that sexy ass car outside, it must be safe to assume that you and he are an item now," Beyonka states nosily.

"It's definitely not safe to assume that," Chamere corrects her. "And he didn't give me the vehicle. I told him I would pay him for it."

"How? Because your bullshit job can't pay for a car that expensive," Erica states factually.

"Unless you're planning to pay it off physically. How much would you charge Liyan an hour to be his on-call plaything?" Beyonka asks amusingly.

Chamere smacks her lips, "Bey, shut up. It's not that kind of exchange, nasty. I told him that I'm only doing real work for him to pay off my debt. It's strictly business."

Beyonka and Erica look at each other. "I hate to break it to you, but Liyan's business is pleasure. To him, both those things go hand and hand," Erica points out accurately.

"Unless she becomes his girlfriend. He's not going to pay for something that he would officially have the rights to," Beyonka adds.

Chamere smacks her lips, "I swear, y'all bitches don't listen. Whether I exclusively date Liyan or not is still up for debate, but I will definitely not be paying for that car with kinky services. Liyan respects me too much to ask me some dumb shit like that, anyway."

CHAPTER FORTY-TWO
Personal Assistant

"How about roleplay," Liyan throws out there, referring to Chamere dressing up for him for money. She is shocked by his request.

"I know you can't be serious," she blurts out. Liyan looks at her amusingly but doesn't respond. She folds her arms, "So, you are really going to stand here and tell me that the job you expect me to do to pay off my debt is to roleplay for you?"

Liyan nods his head, "Yeah, but I would only require you to do it once a week. The only catch is, I need you to be a different person every time I see you."

Fire suddenly burns in Chamere's eyes, "You know what?" She digs in her pocket for the car keys and hurls them towards Liyan's face. He snatches them from mid-air before they hit him. "Keep your fucking car. I don't want it anymore."

"Damn, baby, it was just a joke, sheesh."

She narrows her eyes at him, "Yeah right."

"I'm serious. Do you really think I called you over here to talk about a job and that would be what I came up with? Come on, now… I'm not that horrible."

"You could have fooled me," she spits out.

He shakes his head, "Just follow me." Liyan leads Chamere upstairs and down a hallway she's never been down before. They walk inside the last room on the right. He flicks on the lights in his home office, "Take a seat."

"What's all of this?" Chamere asks, referring to the paperwork laid out before her. He sits down in the chair next to Chamere.

"It's your work contract. I want you to look it over and let me know if you have any questions."

"Personal Assistant?" She inquires after reading the top line.

Liyan nods his head, "Yeah. Since I plan on opening more Club Liquor locations, I'm going to need some help. I'm a smart and thorough guy, but even I have my limits. Besides, two minds are always better than one."

"Well, what would I have to do?"

"Assist me of course, which may look different every day. Like I said, I'm a pretty smart and thorough dude, but there will be times when I need a woman's touch." He glares at her as if his statement had a sexual undertone.

Chamere ignores it, "Wait, it says here that I need to be on-call 24 hours a day. How can I do that, Liyan, when I have another job?"

"You answered your own question… you can't. You're going to have to quit."

Chamere's eyes get big, "Quit? I can't quit."

"Why can't you?"

"Because my job provides me with steady income-"

"This job will, too. Money will be deposited in your account every Friday."

"And I have benefits-"

"On page three, you'll find everything I offer as far as a benefits package is concerned. It's a pretty good package, too. It's far better than the one you're getting at the drugstore." She opens her mouth to reply but he stops her, "And before you ask me how I know, I researched it already. Believe me, I'm giving you a better deal."

She thinks for a minute, "But I thought all of this was about me working to pay for the car, not working to earn a living. I'm not going to be able to do both, Liyan."

"Why won't you be able to do both?" He questions.

"First of all, I have no idea how much I'm supposed to be paying you for the car. Second of all, I have bills and other shit I need to pay for."

"Sounds stressful," he smirks.

She smacks her lips, "Does my impoverished lifestyle entertain you?"

He shakes his head, "I offered to give you the car, Chamere. You created this dilemma yourself."

His words strike her pride. She sighs, "I know, it's just…" she pauses. "I need to compensate you for the vehicle, Liyan. Don't ask me why, but I need to do this."

He sighs this time, "Fine." He points to the bottom of the first contract page, "Did you check out how much you will be making?"

The numbers behind the dollar sign make her eyes nearly pop out her head. She gawks at Liyan, "Are you kidding me? That's for a week?" He nods his head, but she shakes hers, "I can't accept that. That's far too generous."

He stands to move to the other side of his desk. The throne chair he eases in represents the business king that he is, "Don't speak too soon. I plan to get every bit of my money's worth out of your services." She makes a weird face, but he maintains his serious expression, "And only 75% of the number listed will be placed in your checking account. The other 25% will be wired to an escrow account that I will personally oversee. After the car is paid off, then you will receive your full pay."

"You never told me how much I owed you for the vehicle," Chamere points out again.

Liyan leans back in his chair, "Take a look at page seven, first paragraph."

He waits patiently while Chamere searches for the page. She swallows hard after seeing the massive number, "Shit. At this rate, I'll be working for you for the rest of my damn life."

$$$

Liyan spends the remainder of their meeting showing Chamere everything he does on a regular workday. She takes notes as he walks her through the policies and procedures of the club. She tries to maintain her professional composure, but the sight of Liyan's fine ass spitting his business jargon her way is making her hot. She's never met a man as smart and driven as Liyan before. Plus, the way he continuously ignores her sexual glares makes her hot as well.

"Do you have any questions so far?" He asks her after talking for nearly two hours straight.

Chamere shakes her head, "Nope. I believe I have everything down pat."

"Oh, really?" Liyan eases down on the corner of his desk in her direction, "If a customer's membership fee that's paid electronically was declined, then what would I do?"

Chamere flips through her notes before answering, "You would first contact the customer to inform her of the issue. If she's unavailable, you leave a message about non-payment. If she doesn't initiate payment or call back within 24 hours, you activate the color changing mechanism in her card, turning it from gold to white. If there is no payment made by the date of her next payment, her membership would be terminated."

Liyan looks impressed, "Exactly. That's pretty good, Chamere."

She smiles proudly, "Thanks." She pauses, "I do have a question about that, though: Color changing cards? Where on earth did you get technology like that?"

"I met a lot of people in college and some of them were fucking geniuses. This one guy knew everything there was to know about chips in credit cards and debit cards. Low key, he used to activate expired cards all of the time and use them until the companies caught on. That dude was a fucking criminal." Liyan chuckles, "So once I came up with the Club Liquor idea, I reached out to him about creating me a unique membership card that was unlike any other. When he mentioned the idea of color changing cards, I thought he was bullshitting. Turns out, he wasn't."

Chamere processes his words, "So how do they work?"

"I'm not 100% sure of that myself, but he installed software on my computer that changes the color of the card with a click of a button. It's actually pretty dope."

"Was it expensive?"

"Hell yeah it was. I told you, he's a criminal." Chamere snickers and Liyan does, too. "But it was worth the investment. I can tell who paid their membership fees just by glancing at their cards. Club Liquor has grown beyond my wildest dreams because of my attention to details like those. I'm really proud of what I was able to accomplish."

"Oh, so you're proud of profiting off of the pleasure of others, huh?" Chamere teases.

"Ain't all business owners?" He counters. "Think about how you feel when you bite into that burger that you've been craving all day or watch that movie you've been dying to see at the theater. You're excited, happy, and when it's all over, you're satisfied. I provide the same feeling, but my experience is more sensual and hedonistic than the others." He tugs Chamere from her sitting position and holds her in his strong arms. Her skin tingles all over at the feel of his muscular body against hers.

Liyan slowly licks his lips, "Let's use you as an example: You've been fucking me with your eyes nonstop for the past couple of hours. The more I ignored you, the hornier you got… am I right?"

Chamere stares into Liyan's eyes like he's the male lead in her romance movie. She eventually answers, "Yes."

He nods his head, "And now that I'm giving you a small taste of what your body desires, your excitement is growing for me, right?"

"Big time," she mumbles lustfully. He places his lips closely to hers but doesn't kiss her.

"The thought of me getting on my knees and fucking you with my tongue is all you can think about, isn't it? Or is it me bending you over this desk and stroking you until your cum runs down your legs? Which action would make you the happiest?"

"Both of them," Chamere breathes out. Liyan has her so hot and bothered that she can barely think straight.

He smirks, "Well, I guess the only thing left for me to do is satisfy you. Take off your clothes, baby. I'm about to give you exactly what your body needs."

CHAPTER FORTY-THREE
Business Trip

Liyan is a nasty motherfucker, at least that's what Chamere keeps whispering to herself every few seconds. He's currently on his knees in front of her lapping up every juice that oozes out of her vagina. Liyan slurps on her clit like only he knows how to do. He suckles it noisily until she can no longer take it. His entire face is between her pussy lips when she cums. He holds her up with one hand when her legs nearly give out on her.

He looks up at her pleasure-filled face, "Don't fall, baby. Hold on to me. You know I'm not done yet." Liyan eases his butt to the floor and positions Chamere's pussy on top of his hungry mouth. She lowers some of her weight on his tongue like his face is her seat. Chamere's eyes close tightly when Liyan starts to devour her again. She holds the top of his shoulders when he locks on to her spot. Her vibrating legs are no longer giving her the strength she needs to stand. He slides his thick tongue in her vaginal opening and fucks her hard. She gushes down his throat when his tongue's penetration mimics that of a dick.

"Mm…" He moans, allowing her love fluids to run down his chin and dribble on the front of his t-shirt. She moves away from his face the moment he releases her.

"Fuck, Liyan! That was amazing."

He sucks her flavor from his soaked lips, "Don't say was because we're not done yet." Liyan hops to his feet and removes his pants. He positions a naked Chamere across the top of his desk. Her nipples get hard the second they touch the cool wood. Liyan drops his drawers, "Spread em', baby. I'm going in."

Liyan wastes no time sliding inside of Chamere. Her legs tense up the minute he hits her back wall. Liyan strokes her from behind with mighty pumps. It doesn't take him long to hit her g-spot. Chamere knocks several items from his desk once she can no longer take his pounding. She orgasms wildly when he picks up his pace. He growls his way to an orgasm shortly after she does.

"Fuck! Shit!" He exclaims, resting his erupting penis between her ass cheeks. He skeets all over her lower back. He collapses on her instantly afterwards.

"Dammit, Chamere… what are you doing to me?" He questions with his cheek on top of hers.

"What do you mean?" she asks exhaustedly. He slides his dick down her butt crack until it reaches her pussy's entrance. He eases inside of her again. She tries to run from the presence of his overwhelming cock, but the weight of his body keeps her in place. He rolls his hips slow and firm, causing her to cum again in record time.

He talks her through her orgasm, "I've never been this obsessed with a woman before. I don't fuck the same chick more than twice because I know how attached they can get; but you, I'm addicted to fucking you. I can be inside of you and only you for the rest of my life."

Chamere's orgasm finally passes but another one is on its way. She responds before it gets there, "Dammit,

Liyan! I enjoy fucking you, too, but for the rest of your life? That's a hell of a commitment to make."

Liyan moves his hips harder, giving Chamere more of him. She shouts with ecstasy before orgasming again. He sucks on her earlobe, "I know it is, but I mean it. I want you to be mine, baby. I love you, Chamere."

Liyan pumps at Chamere's backside until her cum trickles down her legs, just like Liyan promised it would. She's not sure if it's the moment, or if she's really feeling this way, but she blurts out, "I love you, too."

Liyan pauses after her words, "Are you being serious?"

She thinks for a moment before responding, "I think I am."

He lifts up slightly, "You think or you know?"

She lifts up as well, "I'm not sure, Liyan. Like you said, I think I'm afraid to face how I truly feel about you. All that I know is you mean a lot to me, but whether it's love or not--- only time will tell."

They linger in silence as if neither party knows what to say. Liyan eventually nibbles on Chamere's neck, working his pelvis at the same time. He establishes a sensual rhythm between his sex organ and hers. Chamere bites her bottom lip, "I know one thing, though: I love the way you make my body feel."

Liyan grins while hitting her doggystyle, "Making you fall in love with my sex is the easy part. It's making you fall in love with me that's tricky."

$$$

"I can't quit without giving them my two-week notice, Liyan. That's tacky as hell."

He takes a bite of the food they ordered from the fast-food place down the street. He chews before responding, "It doesn't matter. It's not like you'll be going back to that horrible ass job."

Chamere takes a sip of her soda, "What's so urgent that I need to start working for you tomorrow, anyway?"

"I have a business trip coming up next week that I need my new Personal Assistant to be ready for. If everything goes as planned while we're away, we'll be scouting out locations for a new Club Liquor on the west coast."

Chamere looks excited, "Holy shit, Liyan, that's huge!"

He smiles proudly, "Yeah, it is."

"So, what will we be doing on this trip? And who's going to take care of Club Liquor while you're away?"

"I'll be closing the club until we get back. I already let the ladies' night members know that after Wednesday, we will be closing until further notice. I offered them a month free for the inconvenience." He pauses, "And we have to hit up the other Club Liquor locations so I can discuss my expansion plans with my business partners. First, we're visiting Quan's club and then O'Ryan's."

"It sounds like you're about to lose a lot of money closing both sides of your club," Chamere points out.

"Oh, most definitely, but I'm a smarter businessman than that. The fellas are coming out of town with us, too. They will be making guest appearances at the other Club

Liquors to expose themselves to new clientele. Quan and O'Ryan love to brag about their guys, so I can't wait to show them that my fellas are much better than theirs. I hope we take a few of their customers with us when we leave."

Chamere rolls her eyes, "Great, a battle of the pussy-eaters. Who would have ever thought it?"

Liyan chuckles, "Eating pussy masterfully is an artform… believe me, I know." Liyan licks his lips right after his words. The erotic topic of discussion takes Chamere back to the pleasure Liyan submerged her in a few hours prior. She ignores the sudden throbbing between her legs.

She clears her throat, "Anyway, back to the trip: I need to know how we will be getting there, what day we're leaving, and how long we will be gone."

He smirks as if he can hear her pussy calling his name, "We will be leaving next Friday. I found a nice charter bus for us and the fellas, and I plan on being gone for two weeks or so. That should give us more than enough time to hit Quan and O'Ryan's club. If everything goes as planned, we'll be back before you know it."

Chamere nods her head slowly. She's trying her best to process what's going on, but things are happening so fast with Liyan that it's making her head spin. She has a new luxury car, a new high-paying job, and will soon be on a bus filled with the finest men she's ever known. How will she handle being the only feminine energy on this masculine trip?

She desperately needs to talk her roommates into coming with her.

Liyan stares at her curiously, "What's on that beautiful mind of yours?"

"I was just wondering if it would be OK if I invited Erica and Beyonka with us?" Liyan frowns but doesn't respond. She tries to explain, "It's going to be tough being the only woman on this trip. I would feel much better if I had my girls there to help balance out all of that testosterone. They won't be in the way… I promise."

He appears conflicted, "This is supposed to be a business trip, Chamere, not a vacation. Having guests with us will be a major liability, especially when the guests are dating two of the guys that's going out of town for work. One of the guests is pregnant, too," Liyan shakes his head. "That's more than I'm willing to be responsible for."

"But what if I drove them separately? They will not cause any issues amongst the misters, I swear. I will also keep them far away from Quan and O'Ryan's clubs. That way, the misters can do their jobs efficiently without worrying about their girlfriends hovering over them."

"You're not going to let this go, are you?" Chamere shakes her head no. Liyan sighs, "I guess if you drove separately, it may be able work." Chamere is ecstatic and it shows. Liyan smiles at her reaction, "And to make things easier, I'll pay for the gas in your car, your hotel rooms, and your food."

She is pleasantly surprised, "Oh wow! You went from not wanting them to go to rolling out the red carpet for them."

He bites a fry, "Don't be too flattered. This entire trip is a business expense. Everything I spend will be wrote off on my taxes."

Chamere snickers, "Of course. It's always business with you."

Liyan gawks at her lovingly, "Not always."

She blushes, "I'm starting to see that now."

CHAPTER FORTY-FOUR
Next Stop – Club Liquor: Quan

After wrapping up dinner with Liyan, Chamere rushes home to tell her roommates about the all-expenses paid trip they have coming up with the misters. She busts through the door with an excited stride. Beyonka and Erica are sitting on the couch watching a movie when she barges in. Chamere startles them both.

"Ladies, do I have some news for you."

Erica stands up to join Chamere, "I have some news for you, too." Chamere's demeanor is giddy, but Erica's is more serious.

Chamere looks worried, "OK then, tell me."

"You first," Beyonka butts in to say. She stands next to Erica with the same serious expression. They both stare at Chamere while waiting for her to spill the tea.

"So, remember the other night when we were talking, and we all agreed that we needed a vacation?" Beyonka and Erica nod their heads as if they vaguely remember, "Well, pack your bags, because we're going on a two-week long road trip! We won't have to pay for anything, either. Liyan is taking care of all of our expenses. All you have to do is put in your vacation time at work and we're gone."

Beyonka and Erica are surprised. "Oh wow… a road trip? Where to?" Erica asks.

"I don't know if Dino and Stallion told you, but they have a business trip scheduled for the end of next week. Liyan and the misters will be going to Quan's club and then O'Ryan's club; and since I have to go because I'm Liyan's new Personal Assistant, I talked Liyan into letting y'all go with me."

"Whoa, wait a minute… did you say that you were Liyan's Personal Assistant?" Erica inquires in a shocked tone.

"And Quan and O'Ryan's clubs? So, we're taking a road trip to visit the other Club Liquors?" Beyonka adds, "Because when I said I needed a vacation, that was not what I had in mind."

Chamere tries to explain, "My bad, I'm moving too fast. A lot has happened since the last time I saw y'all."

"We can see that," Beyonka states.

Chamere continues, "Yeah, I'm Liyan's Personal Assistant now, which is kind of weird once you think about it, but the pay and benefits are great." Chamere digs in her purse and pulls out a copy of their contract. She hands it to Erica. She sits down to look over it, "And I know the vacation spots aren't ideal, but ladies, it's free. Picture it: We'll be cruising in my expensive ass vehicle, jamming to our favorite songs, and cracking jokes all the way there. We're not going across state lines for no damn Club Liquors, we're going to see what we can see and eat what we can eat. Besides, your men will be there with us, so they will make sure you have a good time, too. I know it's not our dream getaway, but something is better than nothing, especially if it's free. I say we make the most out of it."

Beyonka nods her head slowly like she understands where Chamere is coming from. Erica rejoins the women after skimming over Chamere's job contract, "Well, you are definitely making more money and getting better benefits than your last job."

Chamere is suspicious of Erica's weird tone, "But…"

"But did you read the part that said you are legally obligated to be Liyan's Personal Assistant for at least two years?"

Chamere nods her head, "Yeah… so? That's how long it should take me to pay off the car. What's wrong with that?"

Erica looks at Beyonka before responding, "Well, don't you think it's a little weird to be working for the man you're in a relationship with?"

Chamere disagrees, "No. I mean, we're not technically together, so…"

"So, you'll be just casually fucking your employer, then? Something like the chef and the clinician are doing?" Beyonka bringing up Keisha and Sharee rubs Chamere the wrong way. She places her hands on her hips.

"That's not the same thing and you know it. Liyan didn't fuck those bitches, he just-"

"Ate their pussies, which is somehow better, I'm assuming," Beyonka interjects sarcastically.

Chamere gets angry, "You know what? I don't get y'all. One minute, you're trying to push me into Liyan's arms and the next minute, you're trying to discourage me from taking advantage of an opportunity of a lifetime. What is the deal with y'all?"

Erica intervenes, "Uh, remember when I said I had something to tell you? Well, it's about Showtime."

"OK…" Chamere mutters, allowing the sound of his name to affect her breathing.

Erica swallows hard, "Dino told me that he finally heard from Showtime and he's doing alright. He said he packed up everything and moved away because there was nothing here for him anymore." Hearing those words is like a hard punch to Chamere's temple. The mental blow knocks her down onto the couch. The other women join her.

"W-What did he mean there was nothing here for him? I'm here," she mumbles, allowing tears to gather in her eyes. "Why would he say that, Erica? I thought we were good friends?"

Erica looks troubled, "Dino didn't go into much detail, but he said that he did tell Showtime you were looking for him, but he made it very clear that he didn't want to be found, especially by you."

That was all Chamere needed to hear to knock the tears from her eyes. Beyonka and Erica take turns consoling her. Chamere wipes her face with her hand, "Why would he say something like that? Why did he leave me without saying goodbye? Where did he go?" Chamere has more questions than Erica has the answers for.

Erica grabs her hand, "According to Dino, he sounded hurt, like something here had broken his heart-"

"Or someone," Beyonka adds in a low tone. Chamere and Erica glare at her. "Come on, y'all, stop playing dumb. We all know what happened, but no one has been woman enough to say it."

"What happened?" Chamere asks, even though she's afraid of Beyonka's blunt answer.

She has her theories, but she's been too scared to entertain them.

"Liyan happened!" Beyonka shouts irritatingly. "You think it's a coincidence that the day you were planning to tell Showtime about Liyan is the day he disappeared? And on top of that, who was waiting outside of your job to whisk you away to his castle in the suburbs immediately afterwards? Didn't you say that was the first night you and Liyan went all the way?" Chamere nods her head yes but doesn't verbalize anything. Beyonka smacks her lips, "Exactly. Liyan ran Showtime away the minute he found out you two had something going on. The situation with you and Liyan broke Showtime's heart. Even though we can't prove it, we all know it's the God's honest truth."

The women sit there in silence after Beyonka's highly probable hypothesis fills their ears. Chamere tries her best to discredit Beyonka's rationale, "Well, that sounds good and all, but until we can talk to Curtis about it, we're just assuming; and like Erica just said, I'm the last person he wants to talk to, so I guess we'll never know."

"Are you sure about that?" Beyonka throws out there.

Chamere appears confused, "Yeah… why shouldn't I be?"

"Actually, there's something else I didn't tell you," Erica blurts out. Chamere stares at her, "Showtime did tell Dino where he moved to. He's just across state lines in a small town in Mississippi. He's working for Quan at his version of Club Liquor, and since we'll be there soon, I'm sure you'll be able to get all of your questions answered once and for all."